M

Fiction Pelev.V

Pelevin, Viktor.

Omon Ra /

JUN   1996

● **O M O N R A**

FARRAR
STRAUS
GIROUX

OMON RA

VICTOR

PELEVIN

Translated from the Russian

by Andrew Bromfield

Farrar, Straus and Giroux

New York

Translation copyright © 1994 by Andrew Bromfield
Published by arrangement with Harbord Publishing Limited, London
All rights reserved
Published simultaneously in Canada by HarperCollins Canada Ltd
Printed in the United States of America
First American edition, 1996

Library of Congress Cataloging-in-Publication Data
Pelevin, Victor.
    [Omon Ra. English]
    Omon Ra / Victor Pelevin.
      p. cm.
    Translated from the Russian.
    I. Title.
  PG3485.E3804613   1996   891.73'44—dc20   95–47618 CIP

The excerpt from an untitled poem by Vladimir Nabokov on page 128 is re-printed by permission of Alfred A. Knopf, a division of Random House, Inc.

For the Heroes

of the Soviet Cosmos

● OMON RA

Omon is not a particularly common name, and perhaps not the best there is. It was my father's idea. He worked in the police all his life and wanted me to be a policeman too.

"Listen to me, Ommy," he used to say to me when he'd been drinking, "if you join the police, with a name like that . . . then if you join the Party . . ."

Although my father had occasionally shot at people, he wasn't really vicious by nature; in his heart he was a cheerful and sympathetic man. He loved me a lot, and hoped that life would at least grant me the achievements it had denied him. What he really wanted was to get hold of a plot of land somewhere near Moscow and start growing beetroot and cucumbers on it—not so that he could sell them at the market or eat them (though that too), but so that he could strip to the waist, slice into the earth with his spade, and watch the red worms and the other underground life wriggling about, so that he could cart barrowloads of dung from one end of the holiday village to the other, stopping at other people's gates to swap a few jokes. When he realised he would never get any of this, he began to hope that at least one of the Krivomazov brothers would lead a long and happy life (my elder brother, Ovir, whom my father had wanted to make into a diplomat, died of meningitis at the age of eleven, and all I remember about him is that he had a long oblong birthmark on his forehead).

My father's plans on my behalf failed to inspire me with any real confidence—after all, he himself was a Party man, and he had a perfectly good Russian name, Matvei, but all he had earned for his efforts was a miserly pension and a lonely, drunken old age.

I don't remember my mother too well. The only memory I have is of my drunken father in his uniform trying to pull his pistol out of its holster while she clutched at his arm, her hair all messed up, and shouted: "Matvei, come to your senses!"

She died when I was still very young, and I was raised by an aunt and went to see my father on weekends. He usually had a red and puffy look, and the medal he was so proud of hung crooked on his soiled pyjama jacket. There was a bad smell in his room, and hanging on the wall was a reproduction of Michelangelo's fresco *The Creation of Adam*, with Adam lying on his back and a bearded God floating above him stretching out his mighty hand to touch the frail human one. This picture had a strangely profound effect on my father; it clearly reminded him of something from the past. I usually sat on the floor of his room and played with a toy train set, while he snored on the fold-down divan. Sometimes he would wake up and peer at me for a while through screwed-up eyes; then he would hang over the edge of the divan, propping himself against the floor, and stretch out a large veinous hand that I was supposed to shake.

"So what's your surname?"

"Krivomazov," I would reply, faking a shy smile, and he would pat me on the head and feed me sweets; he ran through the whole routine so mechanically that it didn't even disgust me.

There's almost nothing I can say about my aunt—she was quite indifferent to me and made sure that I spent most of my free time in various summer camps for Young Pioneers, and extended day-school groups.

Everything I remember from my childhood is linked in one way or another with a dream of the sky. Of course, all this wasn't the very beginning of my life: before this there was a long, bright room full of other children and large plastic cubes scattered haphazardly about the floor; there were the icebound steps of the wooden slide that I plodded up with eager haste; there were the frost-cracked models of young mountaineers made of painted plaster in the yard; and lots more besides. But I can't really say that it was I who saw all this; in early childhood (as, perhaps, after death), a person extends in all directions at the same time, so we can say he still doesn't exist yet—the personality comes into being later, when an attachment to some particular direction appears.

I lived not far from the Cosmos cinema. Our district was dominated by a metal rocket standing on a tapering column of solid titanium smoke, like some huge scimitar thrust into the ground. But funnily enough, it wasn't this rocket that marked the beginning of my personality, it was the wooden aeroplane in the small children's playground beside my block. It wasn't exactly an aeroplane, more a toy house with two windows, and during some repair work someone had nailed on a pair of wings and a tail made from the boards of a fence that had been pulled down, then covered the whole thing with green paint and decorated it with a few large reddish stars. There was room inside for two or three people, and there was a small attic with a little triangular window that looked out onto the wall of the military enlistment office: by unwritten agreement of the entire yard, this attic was regarded as the pilot's cabin, and when the plane was shot down, those who were sitting in the body of the fuselage jumped first, and only afterwards, when the earth was already roaring up towards the windows, could the pilot follow them—if, of course, he had time. I always tried to be the pilot, and I could actually see the sky and the clouds and the earth floating by below, where the brick wall of the military enlistment office should have been, with the whiskery violets and dusty cacti peering forlornly out of its windows.

I really loved films about airmen, and one of these films provided the most powerful experience of my childhood. On a cosmically dark December evening, I switched on my aunt's television and there on the screen was an aeroplane swaying its wings, with an ace of spades on its side and a cross on its fuselage. I leaned down towards the screen, and immediately it was filled with a close-up of the cabin section. Behind the thick panes of glass a subhuman face smiled in goggles like a mountain skier's and a helmet with gleaming ebonite earpieces. The pilot raised an open hand clad in a glove with a long black sleeve and waved to me. Then the screen was filled with an inside view of another plane: two fliers in fur-lined jackets were sitting at iden-

tical control columns and peering through the
metal-framed Plexiglas, following the convolutions of
the enemy fighter flying close beside them.

"M-109," said one flier to the other, "they'll bring us
down." The other, with a handsome emaciated face,
nodded.

"I don't hold it against you," he said, clearly continu-
ing an interrupted conversation. "But just remember:
this thing between you and Varya had better be for life
. . . To the grave!"

At that point I stopped taking in the action on the
screen. I was struck by the sudden thought, or not even
a thought, merely its faintly registered shadow—as
though the actual thought had floated past close to my
head, only catching it with its edge—that if I'd just
been able to glance at the screen and see the world from
the cabin where the two fliers in fur-lined jackets were
sitting, then there was nothing to prevent me from getting into this or any other cabin without the help of the
television, because flight is no more than a set of sensations, the most important of which I'd already learned
to fake, sitting in the attic of the winged hut with the
red stars, staring at the enlistment office wall that was
where the sky should be, and making quiet droning
noises with my mouth.

This vague realisation struck me so hard that I
watched the rest of the film without paying proper attention, getting involved in the television reality only
when the screen was filled with smoke trails or a row of
enemy planes standing on the ground hurtling up towards me. That means, I thought, I can look out from
inside myself like looking out of a plane, it doesn't re-

ally matter at all where you look out from, what matters is what you see . . . From that time on, as I wandered along some wintertime street, I often imagined that I was flying in a plane over snow-covered fields; as I turned a corner, I inclined my head, and the world obediently tilted right or left.

All the same, the person that I could with real certainty call myself took shape only later, and gradually. I think the first glimpse of my true personality was the moment when I realised I could aspire beyond the thin blue film of the sky into the black abyss of space. It happened the same winter, one evening when I was strolling around the Exhibition of Economic Achievements in another corner of Moscow. I was walking along a dark and empty snow-covered alley; suddenly on my left I heard this droning, like a huge telephone ringing. I turned—and saw him.

Sitting there in empty space, leaning back as though in an armchair, he was slowly drifting forwards, and the tubes behind him were straightening out at the same slow pace. The glass of his helmet was black, and the only bright spot on it was a triangular highlight, but I knew he could see me. He could have been dead for centuries. His arms were stretched out confidently towards the stars, and his legs were so obviously not in need of any support that I realised once and for ever that only weightlessness could give man genuine freedom—which, incidentally, is why all my life I've only been bored by all those Western radio voices and those books by various Solzhenitsyns. In my heart, of course, I loathed a state whose silent menace obliged every group of people who came together, even if only for a few seconds, to imitate zealously the vilest and bawdiest individual among them; but since I realised that peace and freedom were unattainable on earth, my spirit aspired aloft, and everything that my chosen path required ceased to conflict with my conscience, because my conscience was calling me out into space and was not much interested in what was happening on earth.

What I saw in front of me was simply a spotlit mosaic on the wall of an exhibition pavilion, a picture of a cosmonaut in open space, but it told me more in an instant than the dozens of books I'd read before that day. I stood there looking at it, until suddenly I felt someone looking at me.

Glancing round, I saw behind my back a rather strange-looking boy my own age—he was wearing a leather helmet with gleaming ebonite earphones, and there were plastic swimming goggles dangling round his neck. He was a little taller than I and probably a few months older. As he entered the area illuminated by the spotlight, he raised an open hand in a black glove, stretched his lips into a cold smile, and for an instant there stood before me the flier from the cabin of that fighter plane marked with the ace of spades.

He was called Mitiok. It turned out that we lived close to each other, although we went to different schools. Mitiok had his doubts about many things, but he knew one thing for certain. He knew that first he would become a pilot, and then he would fly to the moon.

There's obviously some strange correspondence between the general outline of a life and that stream of petty events which a person is constantly involved in and regards as insignificant. I can now see quite clearly that the course of my own life was already set, determined before I had even begun to think seriously about the way I wanted it to turn out: I was even given a glimpse of it in simplified form. Perhaps it was an echo of the future. Or perhaps those things which we take for echoes of the future are actually its seeds, falling into the soil of life at the very moment which in distant retrospect comes to seem like an echo out of the future.

To be brief, the summer after seventh grade was hot and dusty. All I remember of the first half of it are long bicycle rides on one of the highways outside Moscow. I attached a special rattle to the rear of my bike, a Sport semi-racer; it consisted of a piece of thick paper folded over several times and fastened to the frame with a clothes peg—as I rode along, the paper struck against the spokes and made a quick, quiet whirring noise, like the sound of an aero-engine. Time and again as I hurtled down a tarmac incline, I became a fighter plane closing in on its target, and by no means always a Soviet one. But I wasn't to blame for that; it was just that

at the beginning of summer I'd heard someone sing a
stupid song which included the words "Swift as a bullet my Phantom roars into the clear blue sky." I must
confess that for all the song's stupidity, which I realised
perfectly well, I was moved to the depths of my soul.
What other words can I remember? "I see a smoke trail
in the sky . . . My Texas home is far away . . ." And
there was a father, and a mother, and someone called
Mary, a very real person, because she was actually
named in the song.

I was back in Moscow for the middle of July, and
then Mitiok's parents got us places in the Rocket camp.
It was a typical summer camp for children in the south,
maybe even a little better than most. I really only remember the first few days we spent there—but that was
when everything that became so important later happened. In the train Mitiok and I ran through the car-
riages, throwing all the bottles we could find down the
toilets—they fell on the railway tracks rushing by beyond the tiny hatch and burst soundlessly; the stupid
song that was stuck in my head gave this simple game
the flavour of the struggle for the liberation of Vietnam.
The next day the entire contingent for the camp, who
had all travelled in the same train, was unloaded at a
wet railroad station in a provincial town to be counted
and loaded into trucks. We drove for a long time along
a road which looped between mountains; then on our
right the sea appeared and little houses of various colours came drifting towards us. We piled out onto an asphalted parade square and were led up steps flanked by
cypress trees to a low glass-walled building on the top
of the hill. This was the dining hall, where a cold lunch

was waiting for us, although it was already suppertime
—we had arrived several hours later than expected. The
food was pretty bad—thin soup with macaroni stars,
tough chicken with rice, and tasteless stewed fruit.

•

Hanging down from the ceiling of the dining hall on
threads covered with tacky-looking kitchen glue were
cardboard models of spaceships. I stared at one of them
in admiration—the anonymous artist had gone to a
great deal of effort and covered it all over with the letters USSR. The setting sun looking in on it through the
window suddenly seemed to me like the headlight of a
train in the metro as it emerges from the darkness of the
tunnel. Somehow I felt sad.

But Mitiok was in a happy mood and felt like talking.

"In the twenties they had one kind of spaceship," he
said, jerking his fork up into the air, "in the thirties
they were different, in the fifties they were different
again, and so on . . ."

"What kind of spaceships were there in the twenties?" I asked listlessly.

Mitiok thought for a moment.

"Alexei Tolstoy had these huge metal eggs powered
by explosions at minuscule time intervals," he said.
"That was the basic principle, but there could be lots of
variations."

"But they never really flew," I said.

"Neither do these," he answered, pointing to the
model we were discussing as it swayed gently in the
draught.

I finally got his point, although I couldn't really have

put it into words. The only space in which the starships
of the Communist future had flown (incidentally, when
I first came across the word "starship" in the science
fiction books I used to like so much, I thought it came
from the red stars on the sides of Soviet spacecraft) was
the Soviet psyche, just as the dining hall we were sitting in was the cosmic space in which the ships
launched by the previous camp contingent would go on
ploughing their furrows through time up there above
the dining tables, even when the creators of the cardboard fleet were long gone. This thought filtered
through the peculiar indescribable ennui I always suf-
fered after the boiled fruit at the camp, and then I suddenly had a strange idea.

"I used to like making plastic aeroplane models," I
said, "from the kits. Especially military planes."

"So did I," said Mitiok, "but that was a long time
ago."

"I liked the East German kits. But there were no pilots in ours. They looked stupid, because the cockpits
were always empty."

"That's right," said Mitiok. "What made you think of
that?"

"I was just thinking," I said, pointing my fork at the
starship hanging just in front of our table, "whether
there's anyone inside there or not."

"I don't know," said Mitiok. "It's an interesting question, all right."

•

The camp was set on the gentle slope of a hill, and its
lower section formed a kind of park. Mitiok had disap-

peared, and I went off that way on my own; in a few minutes I was in a long, deserted avenue of cypress trees, where it was already half dark.

Wire netting stretched alongside the asphalt footpath, and on the netting there hung large sheets of plywood with hand-drawn posters on them. On the first there was a Young Pioneer with a simple Russian face, staring ahead of him as he pressed a brass bugle with a small flag to his thigh. On the second the same Pioneer had a drum hanging on a strap and was holding the drumsticks. He was there again on the third panel, gazing into the distance in the same way from under a hand raised in salute. The next sheet of plywood was about twice as wide as the rest and very tall—probably about three metres. It was in two colours: on the right, the side from which I was slowly approaching, it was red, and farther away from me it was white, and these two colours were separated by the ragged edge of a wave invading the white surface and leaving a red trail in its wake. At first I couldn't understand what it was, and it was only when I came closer that I recognised the interspersed red and white blobs as the face of Lenin, with a jutting beard that looked like a battering ram, and an open mouth; Lenin had no back to his head—there was just his profile, and all the red surface behind it was Lenin. He was like some incorporeal god rippling across the surface of the world which he had created.

I stumbled over a pothole in the road and shifted my gaze to the next board—it was the Pioneer again, but this time wearing a spacesuit, with a red helmet in his hand; the helmet bore the inscription USSR and a pointed antenna. The next Pioneer was leaning out of a rocket in flight and saluting with a hand in a heavy-duty glove. The final picture was the Pioneer in a space-suit, standing on the cheerful yellow surface of the moon beside a spaceship like the cardboard rocket in the dining hall; all that could be seen of him were his eyes, the same eyes as on the other boards, but because the rest of his face was concealed by the helmet, they seemed filled with some inexpressible anguish.

There was the sound of swift steps behind me, and I turned round and saw Mitiok.

"There *was*," he said, as he came up to me.

"There was what?"

"Look." He held out his hand with something dark lying on the palm. I made out a little plasticine figure with its head wrapped in foil.

"There was a little cardboard chair inside, and he was sitting on it," said Mitiok.

"What, did you take the rocket in the dining hall to pieces?" I asked him.

He nodded.

"When?"

"Just now. Ten minutes ago. The strangest thing of all is that everything in there was . . ." He crossed the fingers of both hands over each other to form a grid.

"In the dining hall?"

"No, in the rocket. When they made it, they started with this little man. They made him and sat him on the chair and glued the cardboard shut all around him."

Mitiok held out a scrap of cardboard. I took it and saw painstakingly detailed drawings of instruments, handles, buttons, and even a picture on the wall.

"But the most interesting thing," Mitiok said in a

thoughtful and depressed sort of voice, "is that there was no door. There was a hatch drawn on the outside, but in the same place on the inside—just some dials on the wall."

I glanced again at the scrap of cardboard and noticed a porthole through which the earth was visible, small and blue.

"I'd like to find the man who stuck this rocket together," said Mitiok. "I'd punch his ugly face for him."

"What for?" I asked.

Mitiok didn't answer. Instead, he swung back his arm in order to chuck the figure over the wire netting, but I caught his hand and asked him to give the figure to me. He didn't object, and I spent the next half hour looking for an empty cigarette pack to use as a case.

•

The echo of this strange discovery came back to us the next day, during the camp's quiet hour. The door opened and Mitiok's name was called; he went out into the corridor. I could hear snatches of conversation, the words "dining hall" were repeated several times, and everything was clear. I stood up and went out into the corridor. Mitiok was there, pressed into the corner by two camp leaders—a skinny young man with a moustache and a squat ginger-haired woman.

"I was there too," I said.

The male leader looked me up and down approvingly.

"Do you want to crawl together or take turns?"

I saw he had a green bag with a gas mask in his hand.

"How can they crawl together, Kolya, when you've

only got one gas mask?" the female leader asked timidly. "They have to take turns."

Mitiok gave me a swift glance and took a step forward.

"Put it on," said the camp leader.

Mitiok put on the gas mask.

"Get down."

He lay on the floor.

"Move," said Kolya, clicking on his stopwatch. The floor of the corridor, which ran the full length of the building, was covered with linoleum, and when Mitiok began to crawl forward, the linoleum gave out a soft but unpleasant squeak. Of course, Mitiok took longer than the three minutes allowed by the camp leader—it wasn't even long enough for him to crawl along the corridor in one direction—but when he had come crawling back towards us, Kolya didn't force him to cover the distance again, because there were only a few minutes left to the end of quiet hour. Mitiok took off the gas mask. His face was red and dripping with tears and sweat. Blisters had swelled up on his feet where they rubbed against the linoleum.

"Now you," said the camp leader, handing me the wet gas mask. "Get ready . . ."

There is something weird and mysterious in the way a corridor looks when you're gazing at its linoleum-spread expanses through the steamed-up lenses of a gas mask. The floor you're lying on chills your belly and chest; you can't even see its far end; the pale ribbon of ceiling and the walls are fused together almost into a point. The gas mask gently squeezes your face, pressing on your cheeks and forcing your lips to stretch into a kind of kiss, apparently addressed to everything around you. Before someone prods you with their foot and orders you to crawl, about twenty seconds pass: a long period of slow torment, time enough to notice all sorts of things. Take the dust—there are several transparent specks there in the crack between two sheets of linoleum; take that painted-over knot in the wood of the skirting board; take that ant that death has transformed into two incredibly thin little petals, which has left behind it a small moist spot in the future half a metre away where the foot of a person walking down the corridor stepped just a second after the disaster.

"Go!" The command rang out above my head and I began cheerfully and earnestly crawling forward. The punishment seemed more like a joke to me, and I didn't understand why Mitiok had turned so weepy. I covered the first ten metres quick as a flash; then it got harder.

When you crawl, there's a moment at which you push off from the floor with the upper part of your foot, and the skin there is thin and delicate; if you've nothing on your feet, you immediately get a blister from the friction. The linoleum stuck to my body, and it felt like hundreds of tiny insects were boring into my legs or like I was crawling over freshly laid asphalt. I was astonished at how slowly time was passing—at one spot on the wall there was a large watercolour of the cruiser *Aurora* in the Black Sea, and I noticed I'd been crawling past it for quite a long time, but it was still hanging there in the same place . . .

Then suddenly everything changed. That is, everything was just the same as before—I was crawling along the corridor in just the same way—but the pain and fa-

tigue, passing beyond the level of endurance, seemed to
switch something off inside me. Or else just the
opposite—they switched something on. I noticed that
all around me it was very quiet, there was only the
squeaking of the linoleum under my feet, as though
something were trundling along the corridor on rusty
castors; outside the windows, way below me, the sea
was murmuring, and somewhere even farther away,
maybe beyond the sea, a loudspeaker was singing with
children's voices.

> *Beautiful yonder, do not hurt me so,*
> *Do not be cruel . . .*

Life was a tender green miracle; the sky was clear and
still, the sun was shining—and in the very centre of
this world stood the two-storey dormitory building, and
inside it was the long corridor, along which I was
crawling in a gas mask. It was all so natural, and at the
same time so painful and absurd, that I began to cry inside my rubber snout, feeling glad that my real face was
hidden from the camp leaders, and especially from the
chinks round the doors, through which dozens of eyes
were gazing at my glory and my shame.

After a few more metres my tears dried up and I
joined in the song, very quietly, maybe without actually
making any sound at all:

> *From the pure source into the beautiful yonder,*
> *Into the beautiful yonder I chart my path.*

The bright brassy note of a trumpet drifted over the camp—that was reveille. I stopped and opened my eyes. There were three metres left to the end of the corridor. On the dark grey wall in front of me hung a shelf, with a yellow globe of the moon standing on it; through the steamy glass smeared with tears it appeared blurred and indistinct, as though it weren't standing on a shelf but hanging in a grey void.

The first time in my life I drank wine was during the winter when I was fourteen. It was in a garage that Mitiok took me to—his brother, a pensive long-haired type who had tricked his way out of army service, worked there as a watchman. The garage was on a large fenced-off lot stacked with concrete slabs, and Mitiok and I spent quite a long time clambering over them, sometimes ending up in astonishing places entirely screened off from the rest of reality which were like the compartments of a long-abandoned spaceship of which only the carcass was left, strangely resembling a heap of concrete slabs. What's more, the streetlamps beyond the crooked wooden fence burned with a mysterious and unearthly light, and a few small stars hung in the pure empty sky —in short, if not for the empty bottles of cheap booze and the frozen streams of urine, we would have been surrounded by cosmic space.

Mitiok suggested going in to warm ourselves up, and we set off towards the ribbed aluminium hemisphere of the garage, which also had something cosmic about it. Inside, it was dark: we could make out the dim forms of cars that smelt of petrol. In the corner was a planking hut with a glazed window, built up against the wall: there was a light on inside it. Mitiok and I squeezed our

way inside, sat down on a narrow, uncomfortable
bench, and silently drank our fill of tea from a battered
tin saucepan. Mitiok's brother was smoking long hand-
rolled cigarettes with cardboard roaches, and looking
through an old issue of *Young Technology* magazine,
and he didn't acknowledge our presence at all. Mitiok
pulled a bottle out from under the bench, smacked it
down onto the cement floor, and asked, "Want some?"

I nodded, although I felt uneasy about it. Mitiok filled
the glass I'd just been drinking tea from right up to the
brim with a dark-red liquid and held it out to me. As
though I was trying to get the hang of some new procedure, I grasped the glass, raised it to my mouth, and
drank, amazed at how little effort was required to do
something for the first time. While Mitiok and his
brother finished off the rest, I paid close attention to my
own sensations, but there was nothing happening to me.
I picked up the magazine that had been put down,
opened it at random, and was faced with a double
spread of drawings of flying machines whose names you
were supposed to guess. I liked one better than the
others—it was an American aeroplane with wings that
could function as a rotor during takeoff—and there was
a small rocket with a cabin for the pilot, but I didn't get
a proper look at that, because without saying a word or
even raising his eyes, Mitiok's brother grabbed the magazine out of my hands. In order not to show I was offended, I moved over and sat at the table, on which a
glass jar with a water-heating element protruding from
it stood among shrivelling pieces of cheap salami.

I suddenly felt disgusted to think that I was sitting in
this lousy little closet that smelt like a garbage dump,

disgusted by the fact that I'd just drunk cheap port from a dirty glass, that the entire immense country in which I lived was made up of lots and lots of these lousy little closets where there was a smell of garbage and people had just been drinking cheap port, and most important of all—it was painful to think that these very same stinking little closets were the settings for those multi-coloured arrays of lights that made me catch my breath in the evenings when I happened to look out of some window set high above the twilit capital. And it all seemed particularly painful in comparison with the beautiful American flying machine in the magazine.

I lowered my eyes to the newspaper which was spread over the table—it was a mass of grease spots, holes burned by cigarette butts, and ring marks left by glasses and saucers. The headlines were strangely frightening, with an inhuman cheerfulness and power: it had been a long time since anyone had stood in their way, but still they went on beating at the empty air, and if you were drunk (and I noticed that I already was, but I didn't attach any importance to it), you could easily just happen to be in the wrong place and get your loitering soul crushed under some MAJOR OBJECTIVE OF THE CURRENT PLAN or some GREETING FROM THE COTTON HARVESTERS. The room around me was suddenly totally strange; Mitiok was watching me carefully. He caught my eye, winked, and, with a tongue that moved thickly, he asked: "What about it, we gonna fly to the moon?"

I nodded, and my eyes came to rest on a small column titled NEWS FROM ORBIT! The bottom of the text had been torn off, and all that was left of the column

were the words "Twenty-eight days . . ." in bold type.
But this was still enough—I understood immediately
and closed my eyes: yes, it was true, perhaps the burrows in which our lives were spent really were dark
and dirty, and perhaps we ourselves were well suited to
these burrows, but in the blue sky above our heads, up
among the thinly scattered stars, there were special, artificial points of gleaming light, creeping unhurriedly
through the constellations, points created here in the
land of Soviets, among the vomit, empty bottles, and
stench of tobacco smoke, points built here out of steel,
semiconductors, and electricity, and now flying through
space. And every one of us, even the blue-faced alco-
holic we had passed on the way here, huddling like a
toad in a snowdrift, even Mitiok's brother, and of course
Mitiok and I—we all had our own little embassy up
there in the cold pure blueness.

I ran outside and stood there for ages, swallowing my
tears as I stared up at the bluish-yellow, improbably
near orb of the moon in the transparent winter sky.

I don't remember the exact moment when I decided to
enroll in military college, probably because this decision had ripened in my soul, and in Mitiok's, long before we graduated from high school. For a little while
we faced the problem of choice—there were a lot of flying schools around the country—but we made our
minds up very quickly once we saw a coloured double-
page insert in the magazine *Soviet Aviation*, all about
life in the Lunar Village at the Maresiev Red Banner
Flying School in Zaraisk. We immediately felt as though
we were there in the crowd of students, among the
yellow-painted plywood mountains and craters; we
could see our future selves in the close-cropped young
men turning somersaults on the gymnastic turnstile and
dousing themselves with the water captured and frozen
by the camera as it fell from a large enamelled basin
that was such a tender peach colour you immediately
remembered your childhood, and somehow the colour
made you trust the picture more and did more to make
you want to go to Zaraisk to study than all the other
photographs of aviation trainers that looked like the
half-decayed corpses of aeroplanes teeming with tiny
people.

Once the decision was made, the rest proved to be

quite easy: Mitiok's parents, puzzled and scared by the
way his brother had turned out, were glad that their
younger son would have such a secure and reliable job.
By this time my father was an inveterate drunkard who
spent most of the time lying on the divan facing the
wall, under a rug embroidered with a goggle-eyed deer:
I don't think he even understood that I intended to be a
flier, while my aunt couldn't have cared less.

•

I remember the town of Zaraisk. Or rather, I can't really
say either I remember it or I've forgotten it—there's so
little in the place either to forget or to remember. Right
in the centre was a tall bell tower of white stone, from
which long ago some princess had leapt onto the stones
below, and despite all the centuries that had passed,
this incident was vaguely remembered by the townspeo-
ple. Next to the tower was the history museum, and not
far from that were the post office and the police station.

When we got out of the bus, a nasty slanting rain was
falling, and it was cold. We huddled under a basement
awning bearing the sign POLLING STATION and waited
half an hour for the rain to pass over. Apparently they
were drinking inside; a strong smell of onions and the
sound of voices came from behind the door. Someone
kept suggesting they should sing, and eventually elderly
male and female voices were raised in song: "Let us re-
joice while we're alive . . ."

The rain stopped; we went to look for the bus and
found the same one in which we'd arrived. It turned
out we need not have got out, we could have waited in

the bus while the driver was having his lunch. Small
wooden houses began drifting past the windows, one after the other; then they stopped and the forest began.
The Zaraisk flying school was in the forest, well away
from the town. It had to be reached by walking about
five kilometres from the final bus stop, which was
called Vegetable Shop (there was no shop anywhere
near, but we were told the name was left over from before the war). Mitiok and I got off the bus and set off
along a road scattered with sodden ash-tree keys; it led
us deeper and deeper into the forest, and just when we
were beginning to think we were going the wrong way,
we suddenly came up against gates made of welded
metal pipes, decorated with large tin stars. On both
sides the forest ran up to a tall fence of grey, unpainted
planks with rusty barbed wire coiling along its top. We
showed the sleepy soldier on gate duty our warrants
from the district military enlistment office and the pass-
ports we had received only recently; we were admitted
and told to go to the club, where a meeting was about
to begin.

Immediately to the right of an asphalted roadway
leading into the centre of a small settlement was the beginning of the Lunar Village I had seen in the magazine
—it consisted of several long, single-storey barracks
buildings painted yellow, surrounded by a dozen or so
tyres dug into the ground, and a special plot designed
to look like a panoramic view of the surface of the
moon. We walked past it and came to the garrison club,
where the boys who had come to enrol were crowded
around the columns. Soon an officer came out, ap-

pointed someone sergeant, ordered us to register with the examination committee and then go and collect our kit.

The examination committee was sitting in a Chinese-looking latticework pavilion in the yard of the club—three officers drinking beer and listening to quiet Eastern music on the radio as they gave out numbered squares of cardboard in exchange for our papers. Then they led us over to the edge of a sports field overgrown with grass that was waist-high (it was obvious no one had played any kind of sport on it for many years) and issued us with two army tents, which we were to live in during the exams. These were rolls of multilayered rubber sheets that we had to stretch out over wooden poles set into the ground. We got to know each other as we dragged the beds into the tents and then set them up in two tiers—the bedsteads were old and heavy, with nickel-plated knobs that could be screwed onto their uprights if they weren't connected with another bed above them. They gave us these knobs separately, in a special bag, and when the exams were over, I secretly unscrewed one and put it away in the cigarette pack where I kept the plasticine pilot with the metal-foil head, the only witness to that distant and unforgettable evening in the south.

We hardly seemed to spend any time at all in the tents, but when they were taken down, there was a dense growth of grass under the rubber groundsheets, colourless and repulsive, with thick stems.

I can hardly remember the actual exams. All I do remember is that they weren't difficult at all, and there was no chance to fill up the answer paper with all the

formulae and graphs that had absorbed the long spring
and summer days we spent poring over the pages of
textbooks. It was no problem for Mitiok and me to get
passing marks, and then came the interview, which
scared everyone more than anything else. We were in-
terviewed by a major, a colonel, and a little old man
with a jagged scar on his forehead, dressed in worn
overalls. I said I wanted to join the cosmonaut class,
and the colonel asked me to define a Soviet cosmonaut.
I thought for a long time, but I couldn't think of the
right answer, and finally I realised from the examiners'
bored expressions that they were about to send me out
into the corridor.

"All right," said the old man, who hadn't spoken a
word before this, "do you remember how you first got
the idea of becoming a cosmonaut?"

I was in despair, because I had no idea how to answer the question. It must have been despair that drove
me to tell him about the red plasticine figure and the
cardboard rocket that had no exit. The old man livened
up straightaway at this, and his eyes began gleaming.
When I got to the part about Mitiok and me having to
crawl along the corridor in gas masks, he even grabbed
hold of my arm and laughed, which made the scar on
his forehead turn bright crimson. Then he suddenly became serious.

"Do you realise how difficult it is to fly into space?"
he asked. "And what if your Motherland requires you to
lay down your life? What then, eh?"

"If it comes to it . . ." I said with a frown.

He stared me right in the eyes for maybe three
minutes.

"I believe you," he said. "You can do it."

When he heard that Mitiok, who had wanted to fly to the moon since he was a baby, was joining too, he noted down his name on a piece of paper. Mitiok told me afterwards that the old man spent a long time asking him why he particularly wanted to go to the moon.

Next day after breakfast, lists of the successful applicants appeared on the columns of the garrison club: my name and Mitiok's were beside each other in the list, out of alphabetical order. Some of the boys trudged off to appeal, some of them jumped up and down for joy on the criss-crossed white lines of the asphalt, some ran to call home, and I recall, high above it all, the white streak of a vapour trail in the colourless August sky.

Those of us who were enrolled as first-year cadets were summoned to a meeting with the flight-training staff—the teachers were already waiting for us in the club. I remember heavy velvet drapes and a table across the full width of the stage, with officers sitting at it looking strict and official. The meeting was chaired by a youthful-looking lieutenant-colonel with a skinny pointed nose: while he was talking, I imagined him in flying suit and pressurised helmet, sitting in the cabin of a MiG fighter covered in blotches, like expensive jeans.

"Okay, boys, we don't want to begin by talking about scary stuff, do we? But you know well enough we don't get to choose the times we live in—the times choose us. Maybe I shouldn't be giving you this kind of information, but I'm going to tell you anyway . . ."

The lieutenant-colonel paused for a second, bent down to the major sitting beside him, and whispered something in his ear. The major grimaced, rapped thoughtfully on the table with his pencil, and then nodded.

"Right," said the lieutenant-colonel in a quiet voice. "At a recent closed session of the political instructors of the armed forces, the times we are living in were defined as a Pre-War Period!"

The colonel paused, waiting for a response, but clearly the audience hadn't understood a thing—at least Mitiok and I hadn't.

"Let me explain," he went on, even more quietly. "The meeting was on July 15, right? So up until July 15 we were living in a Post-War Period, but since then—a whole month already—we've been living in a Pre-War Period. Is that clear or not?"

For a few seconds there was silence in the hall.

"I'm not saying this to scare you," the lieutenant-colonel went on, in a normal voice now, "but we have to remember the responsibility we bear on our shoulders, don't we? And make no mistake about it, by the time you get your diplomas and your ranks, you'll be Real Men with a great big capital M, the kind that exist only in the land of Soviets."

The lieutenant-colonel sat down, straightened his tie, and touched the edge of a glass to his lips—his hands were shaking and I thought I could hear the faintest echo of his teeth rattling against the glass. The major stood up.

"Boys," he said in a melodious voice, "although it would be more correct now to call you cadets, but I'm just going to call you boys anyway. Boys! Remember the story of the legendary hero Alexei Maresiev, immortalised by Boris Polevoi in his book *The Story of a Real Man*! The hero our college is named after! He lost both legs in combat. But after losing his legs, he didn't lose heart, he rose up again on artificial legs and soared into the sky like Icarus to strike at the Nazi scum! Many people told him it was impossible, but he never forgot what was most important—that he was a Soviet man! A Real Man! And you must never forget this, never, wherever you are! All the flight-training staff and I personally, as assistant flight political instructor, promise that we will make Real Men of you in the shortest possible time!"

Then they showed us our places in the first-year cadets' barracks, into which we were being moved from the tents, and took us to the mess hall, where the dusty MiGs and ILs dangling on strings from the ceiling seemed like immense flying islands beside the squadrons of swift black flies.

The dinner was pretty bad: watery soup with macaroni stars, tough chicken with rice, and boiled fruit. After we'd eaten we felt really sleepy; Mitiok and I barely made it to our beds, and I fell asleep straightaway.

The next morning I was awakened by loud groans of
pain and confusion right in my ear. In fact, I'd been
hearing the same sounds in my sleep for a long time,
but I was jerked into full wakefulness only by a particularly loud and piteous wail. I opened my eyes and
looked around. The surrounding beds were alive with a
strange squirming and muffled bellowing—I tried to
prop myself up on my elbow, but I couldn't, because I
was bound to the bed with broad straps like the ones
used to tie up suitcases that are stuffed too full: the
most I could do was turn my head slightly from side to
side. From the next bed I met the pain-filled eyes of
Slava, a young village boy I had got to know the day before; the lower part of his face was hidden by a tightly
tied piece of cloth. I tried to open my mouth to ask him
what was wrong, but discovered that I couldn't move
my tongue, and I had no feeling at all in the lower part
of my face, as though it had gone numb. I guessed that
my mouth must be bound and gagged too, but before I
could feel surprised, I was struck by horror: where Slava's legs should have been, the blanket fell straight
down in an abrupt step, and the freshly starched blanket cover was stained with red blotches like the marks
left on cotton towels by watermelon juice. What was

even more terrifying—I couldn't feel my own legs and I
couldn't lift my head to look at them!

"Platoon 5!" The words thundered out in a sergeant's
fruity bass, replete with an infinitude of allusions. "To
the dressing station!"

About ten men immediately came into the ward—
they were second- and third-year students (or more cor-
rectly, cadets in their second or third year of service, as
I could tell from the stripes on their sleeves). I hadn't
seen them before—the officers had said they were out
helping with the potato harvest. They were wearing
strange boots with tops that didn't bend, and they
walked unsteadily, holding on to the walls or the ends
of the beds. I noticed how pale and unhealthy their
faces were; they seemed to bear the imprint of long
days of interminable torment, to have been recast in a
fixed expression of readiness. Inappropriately enough,
at that moment I recalled the words of the Young Pioneers' greeting Mitiok and I had repeated with all the
others on the distant parade square at summer camp—
and I realised just what frauds we'd been, loudly assur-
ing ourselves, our comrades in the lineup, and the
transparent July morning that we were "always
prepared".

The cadets wheeled the beds out into the corridor one
after another, with the first-years bound down on them
moaning and squirming, until only two were left in the
room—mine and one by the window, on which Mitiok
was lying. I couldn't get a proper look at him because of
the straps, but I could see out of the corner of my eye
that he was quiet and seemed to be asleep.

They came for us about ten minutes later, turned us

round, feet first, and wheeled us along the corridor. One
cadet pushed the bed while another walked backwards
and pulled it towards him; it looked as if he were back-
ing down the corridor and warding off the bed as it pur-
sued him. We trundled into a long, narrow lift with
doors at both sides and went up, the second-year stu-
dent backed away from me down another corridor, and
we stopped beside a door upholstered in black with a
large brown plaque that I couldn't read because of my
uncomfortable position. The door opened, and I was
rolled into a room with an immense crystal chandelier
in the shape of an aircraft bomb hanging from the ceiling; the upper section of the walls was decorated with a
band of bas-relief ornamentation made up of sickles,
hammers, and urns entwined with grapevines.

They took my straps off, and I propped myself up on
my elbows, trying not to look at my legs: straight ahead
of me at the back of the room a green lamp stood on a
massive desk that was illuminated by the slanting grey
light from a tall narrow window. The person sitting at
the desk was hidden from me by the open pages of a
copy of *Pravda*, from the front of which a wrinkly face
with radiantly kind eyes stared straight at me. The lino
on the floor squeaked, and Mitiok's bed came to a halt
beside mine.

The newspaper rustled a few times as its pages were
turned, and then sank down onto the table.

There in front of us was the little old man with the
scar on his forehead, the one who had grabbed me by
the arm during the interview. Now he was wearing the
uniform of a lieutenant-general with brocade at the but-
tonholes, his hair was neatly brushed down, and his

gaze was clear and sober. I noticed that his face seemed like a copy of the one that had been looking at me from the front page of *Pravda* just a minute before: it was just like in a film I saw, where they showed one icon for a long time, and then another one gradually appeared in its place—the images were similar, but not quite the same, and because the transition was blurred, it seemed as if the icon were changing in front of your eyes.

"Now, boys, since you and I will be seeing quite a lot of each other for quite a long time, you can call me Comrade Flight Leader. Allow me to congratulate you on the results of your exams—and the interview in particular," said the old man, winking. "You have been registered immediately for the first-year course at the KGB secret space-training school—so you'll just have to wait a bit before you become Real Men. Meanwhile, get ready to go to Moscow. I'll see you there."

I didn't realise what he'd said till we'd been taken back to the empty ward along those long corridors, where the lino sang a quiet song of nostalgia beneath the tiny casters of the bed, reminding me somehow of a day in July by the sea.

Mitiok and I slept the whole day (it seems they'd drugged our supper the previous evening—I was still sleepy the next day), and that evening a jolly yellow-haired lieutenant in squeaky boots came for us, and laughed and cracked jokes as he wheeled our beds out onto the asphalt parade ground in front of the platform with the concrete shell-shaped canopy, where several senior generals with kind intelligent faces, including Comrade Flight Leader, were sitting at a table. Of course, Mitiok and I could have walked there on our own, but the lieutenant said that this was standing orders for first-year cadets, and he ordered us to lie still so as not to upset the others.

All those beds stacked up against one another made the parade ground look like the yard of an automobile factory or a tractor plant: a subdued groaning traced a complex flight path above it—dying away in one place, it sprang up in another, and then in a third, as though some huge invisible mosquito were darting about above the beds. On the way out, the yellow-haired lieutenant told us that a combined graduation party and final state exam was about to begin.

Soon we were watching our lieutenant, the first of about fifty like him, as he danced the "Kalinka" for the exam committee. He was pale and nervous, but he performed with incomparable mastery, to the sparse accompaniment of the assistant political instructor's accordion. The lieutenant was called Landratov—I heard his name when the Flight Leader handed him a red diploma and congratulated him on receiving it. Then the same dance was performed by all the others, and by the end I was bored stiff watching them. I turned to look at the sports field immediately beside the parade ground—and suddenly realised why it lay under such a thick covering of wild grass.

I lay there and watched the stems swaying in the wind. The grey, rain-cracked fence topped with barbed wire just beyond the ruined soccer goalposts seemed to me like the Great Wall, still stretching, despite all the warped and missing planks, all the way from the fields of distant China to the town of Zaraisk, making everything that appeared against its background look ancient and Chinese—the latticework pavilion where the exam committee worked, the obsolete fighter plane, and the ancient army tents I could see from where I lay on my bed, clutching in my fist the nickel-plated knob I'd unscrewed for a souvenir.

The next day a truck carried Mitiok and me off through the summery woods and fields: we sat on our rucksacks, leaning against the cool steel of the side of the truck. I remember the edge of the tarpaulin swaying, and beyond it glimpses of tree trunks and grey, dried-out telegraph poles from which the wires had long since been torn down. From time to time the trees parted and I glimpsed a pale, pensive triangle of sky. Then there was a halt and five minutes' silence, punctuated only by a dull, distant rattling; the driver, who had got out to relieve himself, explained that they were firing short bursts on the one or two machine guns they had at the shooting range close by. Then it was back to the truck's interminable jolting: I fell asleep, and woke up again for a few seconds only when we were already in Moscow, as the chink in the tarpaulin revealed a glimpse of a sight from some long-ago summer of my schooldays—the archways of the shop Children's World by the Lubyanka.

As a child I often used to imagine an open newspaper, still smelling of fresh ink, with a large portrait of myself right in the centre (wearing a helmet and a smile), and the caption: "Cosmonaut Omon Krivomazov feels just fine!" It's not easy to understand just why I wanted this so badly. Maybe I was dreaming of living part of my life through other people—the people who would look at this photograph and think about me, and try to imagine what I thought and felt, the inner workings of my soul. Most important of all, perhaps, I wanted to become one of these people myself—to stare at my own face, made up of thousands of typographic dots, and wonder what kinds of films this man likes, and who his girlfriend is, and then suddenly remember that this Omon Krivomazov is me. Since then I've changed, gradually and imperceptibly. I've stopped being interested in other people's opinions, since I realised that other people wouldn't be interested in me anyway; they wouldn't be thinking about me but about my photograph, and with the same indifference I feel for other people's photographs. So the news that my heroism would remain unknown was no blow to me. The blow was the news that I would have to be a hero.

Mitiok and I were taken by turns to see the Flight

Leader the day after we arrived, as soon as we were kit-
ted out in black uniforms, with bright yellow epaulettes
bearing the incomprehensible initials HSS. Mitiok went
first, and I was called an hour and a half later.

When the tall oak doors first opened to admit me, I
was astounded how closely the room resembled a scene
from some war film. In the centre of the office stood a
table covered with a big yellow map, with several men
in uniform standing round it: the Flight Leader, three
generals, and two colonels, one a short fat man with a
bright scarlet face and the other a skinny man with
thinning hair who looked like an aging sickly little boy
—he was wearing dark glasses and sitting in a
wheelchair.

"Commander of Central Flight Control Colonel Khalmuradov," said the Flight Leader, pointing at the fat
man with the red face.

Khalmuradov nodded.

"Assistant Political Instructor of the Special Cosmonauts' Detachment Urchagin."

The colonel in the wheelchair turned his face towards
me, leant forward in a slight bow, and removed his
glasses, as if to take a closer look at me. I couldn't help
shuddering—he was blind; the lids of one eye had completely fused together, and whitish mucus gleamed
dully between the lashes of the other.

"You may call me by my first name, Bamlag," he said
in a high tenor voice. "I hope we're going to be friends,
Omon."

The Flight Leader didn't introduce me to the generals,
and nothing in their behaviour indicated that they even
noticed I was there. I thought, though, that I'd seen one

of them during the examinations at the Zaraisk flying
school.

"Cadet Krivomazov," said the Flight Leader, introduc-
ing me. "Well, shall we begin?"

He turned towards me, folded his hands on his belly,
and said: "Omon, I'm sure you read newspapers and
watch films, and you know that the Americans have
landed some of their astronauts on the moon and even
driven around up there in a motor carriage. Their goals
are supposedly peaceful, but that all depends on how
you look at things. Just imagine a simple working man
from some small country—say, in Central Africa . . ."

The Flight Leader wrinkled up his face and went
through the motions of rolling up his sleeves and wip-
ing the sweat from his brow.

"And then he sees that the Americans have landed on
the moon, while we . . . You understand?"

"Yes, sir, Comrade Lieutenant-General!" I replied.

"The main purpose of the space experiment for which
you will now be prepared, Omon, is to demonstrate that
we do not lag behind the countries of the West in technology and that we are also capable of sending expedi-
tions to the moon. At the moment it is beyond our
capability to send a piloted, recoverable ship. But there
is another possibility—we can send an automated ves-
sel, which will not have to be brought back."

The Flight Leader leaned over the protruding mountains and small hollow craters of the relief map. A
bright red line cut across its centre, like a fresh scratch
made with a nail.

"This is a sector of the lunar surface," said the Flight
Leader. "As you know, Omon, our space science pro-

gramme has mostly studied the far side of the moon, whereas the Americans landed on the bright side. This long line here is the Lenin Fissure, discovered a few years ago by one of our sputniks. Last year an automated expedition was sent to this unique geological formation to gather samples of the lunar surface, and the initial analyses have suggested that further investigation of the fissure is required. No doubt you know that our space programme is oriented mostly towards automation —it's the Americans who risk human lives. We expose only machines to danger. The idea is to send a special self-propelled vehicle, a so-called moonwalker, which will travel along the bottom of the fissure and transmit scientific information back to earth."

The Flight Leader opened the drawer of his desk and began rummaging about in it with his hand, keeping his eyes on me all the while.

"The overall length of the fissure is one hundred and fifty kilometres, but its width and depth are a matter of a mere few metres. It is proposed that the moonwalker will travel along it for seventy kilometres—the batteries should have enough power for that distance—and set up a radio buoy at its centre point, which will broadcast into space radio waves encoding the words 'Peace', 'Lenin', and 'USSR'."

A small red toy appeared in his hand. He wound it up and set it at the beginning of the red line on the map. The toy began to buzz and edged forward—its fuselage was like a tin can set on eight small black wheels, with the letters USSR on its side and two eye-like bulges at the front. Everyone followed its motion intently; even Colonel Urchagin turned his head in time with the others. The toy reached the edge of the table and tumbled onto the floor.

"Something like that," the Flight Leader said thoughtfully, casting a quick glance at me.

"Permission to speak, sir?" I heard my own voice.

"Fire ahead."

"Surely the moonwalker is automated, Comrade Lieutenant-General?"

"It is."

"Then what am I needed for?"

The Flight Leader lowered his head and sighed.

"Bamlag," he said, "your turn."

The wheelchair's electric motor hummed, and Colonel Urchagin moved away from the table.

"Let's go for a little walk," he said, driving over and taking hold of my sleeve.

I glanced enquiringly at the Flight Leader. He nodded. I followed Urchagin out into the corridor, and we began walking slowly along—that is, I walked and he rode beside me, adjusting his speed with a lever which was topped by a homemade Plexiglas ball with a carved red rose inside it. Several times Urchagin opened his mouth and was about to speak, but each time he closed it again, and I was already sure he didn't know where to begin, when he suddenly grabbed my wrist in his narrow hand.

"Listen carefully now, Omon, and don't interrupt," he said with feeling, as though we'd just been singing songs together round the campfire. "I'll start with the general background. You know, the fate of humanity is full of tangled knots, things that don't seem to make any sense, bitter realities hard to accept. You have to see things very clearly, very precisely, in order not to make too many mistakes. Nothing in history is like it is in the textbooks. Dialectics led to Marx's teaching, which was intended for an advanced country but won its victory in the most backward one. We Communists had no time to prove the correctness of our ideas—the war cost us too much of our strength, we had to spend too long struggling against the remnants of the past and our enemies within the country. We just didn't have the time to defeat the West technologically. But in the battle of ideas, you can't stop for a second. The paradox—another piece of dialectics—is that we support the truth with falsehood, because Marxism carries within itself an all-conquering truth, and the goal for which you will give your life is, in a formal sense, a deception. But the more consciously . . ."

I felt my heart sink, and I tried spontaneously to pull my wrist free, but Colonel Urchagin's fingers seemed to have turned into a narrow hoop of steel.

". . . the more consciously you perform your feat of heroism, the greater will be the degree of its truth, the greater will be the meaning of your brief and beautiful life!"

"Give my life? What heroism?" I asked in a faint voice.

"Why, the very same heroism," he said equally quietly, sounding as though he was frightened, "that has already been demonstrated by more than a hundred young lads just like you and your friend."

He said nothing for a moment, and then continued in his former tone of voice: "You've heard it said that our space programme is based on automated technology?"

"Yes."

"Let's you and me go to room 329, and they'll tell you about our space automation techniques."

"Comrade Colonel!"

"Comrade Camel!" he echoed, mocking me. "They asked you at Zaraisk if you were willing to give your life, didn't they? What answer did you give?"

I was sitting in an iron chair bolted to the floor in the centre of the room; my arms were clamped to the armrests, my legs to the chair's legs. The windows were covered with thick blinds, and in the corner there was a small writing desk with a telephone without a dial. Colonel Urchagin was sitting opposite me in his wheelchair; as he spoke he laughed, but I could tell he was deadly serious.

"Comrade Colonel, you must understand, I'm just an ordinary boy. You think I'm some kind of great . . . But I'm not one of those people who . . ."

Urchagin's wheelchair hummed as he began to move. He came right up close to me and stopped.

"Wait a moment, Omon," he said, "wait a moment. Now we're getting to the point. Just whose blood do you think the soil of this country of ours is watered with? Some kind of special blood, perhaps? From some kind of special people?"

He reached out a hand, felt my face, and then struck me across the mouth with his dry little fist—not really hard, just hard enough for me to feel the taste of blood in my mouth.

"That's the kind of blood it's watered with. From lads like you . . ."

He patted me on the neck.

"Don't be angry," he said. "I'm your second father now. I can even take my belt to you. Why are you cringing like a woman?"

"I don't feel ready to be a hero," I answered, licking away the blood. "That is, I feel I'm definitely not ready . . . I'd rather go back to Zaraisk than . . ."

Urchagin leaned towards me and stroked my neck as he spoke in a soft and gentle voice.

"Don't be such a little fool, Ommy. You should know, my son, that that's what heroism is all about. No one's ever ready to be a hero—there's no way to prepare for it. Of course, you can practise till you're really good at running up to the gunport and have the knack of falling neatly across it on your chest—we teach all of that. But you can't teach anyone the actual inner act of heroism, it can only be performed. The more you wanted to live before, the better for the act of heroic sacrifice. The country needs heroic feats, even invisible ones—they nourish that fundamental strength which . . ."

I heard a loud croaking sound. The black shadow of a bird flitted across the blinds, and the colonel fell silent. He pondered for a while in his wheelchair, then switched on the motor and trundled out into the corridor. The door slammed behind him and then opened again a moment later to admit a yellow-haired air force lieutenant carrying a length of rubber hose. His face

looked familiar, but I couldn't figure out where I'd seen
him before.

"Recognise me?" he asked.

I shook my head. He went over to the table and sat
on it, his legs dangling down in their gleaming black
boots with concertina folds, at the sight of which I remembered where I'd seen him—he was the lieutenant
from the Zaraisk flying school who had wheeled my
bed and Mitiok's out onto the parade ground. I even remembered his name.

"Lan . . . Lan . . ."

"Landratov," he said, flexing the rubber hose. "I've
been sent to have a talk with you. Urchagin sent me.
You don't really want to go back to the Maresiev
School, do you?"

"It's not that I want to go back there," I said. "I don't
want to go to the moon. To be a hero."

Landratov chuckled and slapped his hands on his
belly and his thighs.

"Well now," he said, "so you don't want to? D'you
think they'll leave you in peace now? Or just let you
go? Or send you back to the school? And even if they
do, have you got any idea what it's like when you get
up from your bed and take your first steps on crutches?
Or how it feels before the rain?"

"No," I said.

"Or maybe you think when your legs heal up it's a
bed of roses? Last year two cadets were tried for state
treason. From the fourth year they work on flight
simulators—d'you know what those are?"

"No."

"Basically it's just like being in a plane: you sit in a cockpit with your control column and your pedals—only you're watching a television screen. So this pair of swine, instead of practising their Immelman loops, flew off west at minimal height and refused to respond to the radio. When they eventually dragged them out, they asked them what they thought they had been up to. Neither of them would say anything, but one answered the question later. Said he just wanted to feel what it was like, didn't he, just for a minute . . ."

"And what happened to him?"

Landratov smacked the rubber hose down on the table beside him.

"What's it matter?" he said. "The main thing is, I can understand them. All that time you keep hoping that eventually you'll get around to flying, so when they finally tell you the truth . . . D'you think anyone needs you without legs? And the country's hardly got any planes, they just fly up and down the borders so the Americans can photograph them. And even then . . ."

Landratov fell silent.

"Even then?"

"Never mind. What I wanted to say was, d'you think that after Zaraisk you'd be hurtling through the clouds in a fighter plane? If you were lucky, you might just find yourself in a song-and-dance ensemble in some air-force defence district. But most likely you'd end up dancing the 'Kalinka' in some restaurant. A third of us take to drink, and another third—the ones whose operation didn't go right—end up committing suicide. How d'you feel about suicide, anyway?"

"I don't really know," I said. "I never thought about it."

"Well, I used to think about it. Especially during the second year, when they were showing tennis on the TV and I was on duty in the club with my crutches. I was real miserable. And then it passed. Once you can come to terms with yourself, it gets easier. So you just remember, if you get any thoughts like that, not to give in. You should be thinking about all the interesting things you'll see if you go to the moon. These buggers won't let you go alive, anyway. Better play along with them, okay?"

"You don't seem to like them much," I said.

"What's there to like them for? Every word they say is a lie. Which reminds me, when you're with the Flight Leader, don't you mention anything about dying, or even about you flying to the moon. Just talk about automatic systems, okay? Or we'll be having another little talk in this room. I follow orders."

Landratov swung his rubber hose through the air; then he took a pack of Flight cigarettes from his pocket and lit up.

"That friend of yours agreed straightaway," he informed me.

•

When I went out into the air, my head was spinning slightly. The inner yard, separated from the city by the grey-brown blocks of the building, was very much like a part of a country village that had been cut out precisely to fit the yard and then transported here: there was a wooden summerhouse with cracked and peeling paint, and a horizontal bar welded together out of iron pipes, with a strip of green hallway carpet hanging on it— someone must have been beating it and then forgotten it; there were allotments, a chicken coop, and a sports field, several table-tennis tables, and a circle of old painted tyres half buried in the ground that immediately reminded me of photographs of Stonehenge. Mitiok was sitting on a bench by the exit. I went over and sat beside him, stretched out my legs, and looked at the black uniform trousers tucked into my boots—after the conversation with Landratov I felt as though the legs in them weren't really mine.

"Is it all true?" Mitiok asked in a quiet voice.

I shrugged. I didn't know exactly what he meant.

"All right, I can believe the stuff about the aeroplanes," he said. "But all that about the nuclear weapons . . . Maybe back in '47 you could still make two million political prisoners all jump at once. But we don't have them anymore, and there are nuclear tests every month . . ."

The door I had just come out of opened, and Colonel Urchagin's wheelchair drove out; he braked and surveyed the yard several times with his ear. I realised he was looking for us in order to add something to what had already been said, but Mitiok stopped speaking, and Urchagin obviously decided not to bother us after all. The wheelchair's electric motor hummed and it moved away to the opposite wing of the building. As he rode past us, Urchagin turned his smiling face in our direction and the sunken hollows of his eyesockets seemed to peer benevolently into our very souls.

I think most Muscovites know perfectly well what's going on deep below their feet during those hours when they're queuing at the Children's World department store next to the KGB building or when they ride the metro through Lubyanka station, so I won't go over it all again. Let me simply say that the model of our rocket was full-size and there was room for another one just as big beside it. The lift was an old prewar model that took so long getting down that you could read two or three pages of a book on the way.

The model rocket was a rather patchy construction, with parts of it just knocked together from planks, and only the crew members' workplaces were precise recreations of the real thing. It was all intended for practical training, which Mitiok and I would not begin for some time yet. Even so, we were moved straight into a spacious box down below, with two pictures pretending to be windows presenting a panoramic view of Moscow under construction.

There were seven beds, so Mitiok and I knew our numbers would soon be increasing. The box was only three minutes' walk along a corridor from the training hall where the model rocket stood. An interesting thing seemed to happen to the lift—whereas before it had

seemed to take a long time to go down, now it seemed
to take even longer to go up.

We didn't go up very often, since we spent most of
our free time in the training hall. Colonel Khalmuradov
gave us a brief series of lectures on the theory of rocket
flight, using the model rocket to illustrate his points.
When we were studying the technical equipment, the
rocket was simply a study aid, but when evening came
and the main lights were turned off, sometimes, for a
few seconds, the dim wall lamps transformed it into
something long forgotten and wonderful, a final greeting
to Mitiok and me from our childhood.

·

He and I were the first to arrive. The other members of
our crew appeared in the college over a period of time.
The first was Sema Anikin, a short stocky village lad
who had been a sailor. The black uniform really suited
him—unlike Mitiok, who looked like a scarecrow in it.
Sema was very calm and didn't speak much and spent
all his time on training, as all of us should have done,
although his job was the simplest and the least romantic. He was responsible for the rocket's first stage, and
his young life, in the words of Urchagin, who loved
pompous and convoluted phrases, was destined to be
broken off a mere three minutes after takeoff. The suc-
cess of the entire expedition depended on the precision
with which he performed his task, and if he made the
slightest mistake, we would all face an early and senseless death. Sema obviously laboured under the burden
of this responsibility, and he even trained in the empty
barracks, honing his movements till they were com-

pletely automatic. He squatted down, closed his eyes, and began moving his lips as he counted up to 240, and then he began turning anticlockwise, performing complicated hand movements every forty-five degrees. Even though I knew he was mentally opening the catches that attached the first stage to the second, his movements reminded me every time of something out of a Hong Kong martial-arts movie; having gone through this complex manual procedure eight times, he immediately fell on his back and kicked upwards powerfully with both legs, thrusting against the invisible second stage.

Our second stage was Ivan Grechka, who arrived about two months after Sema. He was a Ukrainian with light hair and blue eyes, who was transferred to us from the third year at Zaraisk, so he still walked with some difficulty. He had a certain kind of warm simplicity, as though he was always smiling at the world, and everyone he met loved him for this smile. Ivan became particularly close friends with Sema. They teased each other all the time and were constantly competing to see who was quicker and better at running through the operations to detach his stage. Sema was nimbler, but Ivan had to open only four catches, so sometimes he was quicker.

Our third stage, Otto Plucis, was a ruddy-faced meditative Balt. As far as I can recall, he never once joined Ivan and Sema when they were practising in the barracks—he always seemed to be lying on his bunk doing the crosswords in *Red Warrior*, his legs in their painstakingly polished boots crossed on the gleaming nickel-plated bar of the bedstead. But you only had to see how he dealt with his share of the catches on the model to realise that if there was one reliable section in our rocket, then it was the separation system for the third stage. Otto was a funny guy. After the all-clear, he enjoyed telling stupid stories like the ones children tell to frighten each other at summer camp.

"Once, this expedition flies off to the moon," he would say in the darkness. "They've been flying for ages, and they're just getting close. Then suddenly the hatch opens and in come some people in white coats. The cosmonauts say: 'We're flying to the moon!' The people in white coats say: 'Fine, fine. No need to get excited. We'll just give you this little injection . . .' "

•

Mitiok and I still hadn't begun technical equipment training when the training for the ballistics group was made more complicated. It hardly affected Sema Anikin —his feat of heroism took place at a height of four kilometres, and all he had to do was put on a padded work jacket over his uniform. It was harder for Ivan: at forty-five kilometres, where his moment for immortality arrived, it was cold, and the air was already rarefied, so he trained in a sheepskin coat, tall fur boots, and an oxygen mask, which made it difficult for him to climb in through the narrow hatch on the model. Otto had things easier—a special spacesuit was made for him, complete with electrical heating. It was sewn by the seamstresses at the Red Mountain clothing factory from several American high-altitude suits captured in Vietnam, but it wasn't quite ready yet—they were still finishing off the heating system. In order not to lose time, Otto practised in a deep-sea diver's suit; I can still see his red, sweaty,

pockmarked face behind the glass of the helmet as it
rose out of the hatch; when he said hello, the friendly
words came out as strangely jumbled sounds.

•

The lectures on the general theory of automated cosmic
systems were read to us in turn by the Flight Leader
and Colonel Urchagin.

The Flight Leader was called Pkhadzer Vladlenovich
Pidorenko. He got his name from the small Ukrainian
village where he was born. His father had been in the
Cheka too, and following the fashion of those days, he'd
taken his son's first name from the first letters of the
Russian words for "Party and Economic Activists of the
Dzerzhinsky District", while his second was an abbrevi-
ation of "Vladimir Lenin": what's more, if you added
up the letters in the two names Pkhadzer and Vladlen,
there were fifteen, the same as the number of Soviet re-
publics. But he couldn't stand being called by his own
name, and subordinates who served with him called
him either Comrade Lieutenant-General or, like myself
and Mitiok, Comrade Flight Leader. He pronounced the
phrase "automated systems" with such pure, visionary
intonation that for a second his office in the Lubyanka,
which we went up to for his lectures, was transformed
into the sounding board of some immense grand piano
—but even though the phrase turned up in his speech
quite often, he gave us absolutely no technical information, and spent most of the time telling us run-of-the-
mill stories or reminiscing about his wartime days with
the partisans in Belorussia.

Urchagin didn't deal with any technical topics, either.

He usually nibbled on sunflower seeds, laughing as he spat out the shells, or told us jokes.

"How do you divide a fart into five parts?" he asked once.

When we said we didn't know, he answered himself: "Fart into a glove."

And he would burst into thin laughter. I was amazed at the positive optimism of this man, blind, paralysed, chained to a wheelchair, but nonetheless carrying out his duty and never tiring of life. There were two political instructors in the space school who were very like each other—Urchagin and Burchagin, both colonels. It was Urchagin who usually taught our crew. There was only one Japanese wheelchair with an electric motor for the two of them, so when one of them was busy with educational work, the other would lie silent and motionless, propped up on his elbow on the bed in a tiny room on the fifth floor, wearing his uniform jacket and covered up to the waist with a blanket that hid the bedpan from probing eyes. The poor furnishings of the room—a map case for writing on, with narrow slits in the sheet of cardboard laid over it, a glass of strong tea permanently on the table, the white curtain and the rubber plant—all touched me so profoundly I almost wept, and at those moments I stopped thinking that all Communists were cunning, mean, and self-serving.

•

The last member of the crew to arrive was Dima Matiushevich, who was responsible for the lunar module. He was very withdrawn and, despite his young years, quite grey. He kept himself to himself, and all I knew

about him was that he'd served in the army. When he
saw the reproduction of a painting by Kuindzhi that Mitiok had cut out of a magazine and hung over his bed,
he hung a sheet of paper over his own bed, with a
small drawing of a bird and three words in big block
capitals: OVERHEAD THE ALBATROSS.

Dima's arrival coincided with the introduction of a
new discipline into the timetable, known as "Strong in
Spirit". It wasn't really a study subject in the normal
sense of the word, although it was given pride of place
on the timetable. We began to get visits from people
who were professional heroes—all of them told us
about their lives without a trace of sentimentality; their
words were the same simple ones you heard in the
kitchen at home, so the very essence of their heroism
seemed to spring from the ordinary, from the petty details of everyday life, from the grey, cold air around us.

The person I remember best of all from "Strong in
Spirit" is retired Major Ivan Trofimovich Popadya—a
funny kind of name. He was tall, a real Russian Hercules, and his jacket was festooned with medals. His face
and neck were red, and dotted all over with small white
scars. He wore a patch over his left eye. His life was
very unusual: He began as a simple huntsman in a
hunting reserve used by Party leaders and members of
the government, and his duties were to drive the
animals—wild boar and bears—towards the marksmen
hiding behind the trees. One day there was a terrible accident. A big male boar broke across the line of flags
and fatally injured a Party leader who was firing from
behind a birch tree. He died on the way to the nearby
town, and a session of the supreme organs of power

adopted a resolution forbidding the leadership to hunt wild animals. But, of course, the need remained, and one day Popadya was summoned to the Party Committee of the hunting reserve, where they explained the whole business to him and then said: "Ivan! We can't order you to do it—and even if we could, we wouldn't, not this. But it's something that needs to be done. Think about it. We won't force you."

Popadya thought hard about it all night long, and next morning he went to the Party Committee and said he agreed.

"We didn't expect any other answer," said the Party Secretary.

They gave Ivan a bulletproof waistcoat, a helmet, and a boar skin, and he went to work at his new job—a job which it would be no exaggeration to describe as daily heroism. For the first few days he felt a little afraid, especially for his exposed legs, but then he got used to it, and the members of the government, who all knew what was going on, tried to aim at his side, at the bulletproof waistcoat, which Ivan padded with a small pillow to soften the impact. Occasionally, of course, some old codger from the Central Committee would miss his aim, and then Ivan would go on extended sick leave and read a lot of books, including his favourite, the memoirs of the famous flier Pokryshkin. Just how dangerous this work was—every bit as bad as active military service—can be judged from the fact that every week they had to replace Ivan's bullet-riddled Party card, which he carried in the inside pocket of the boar skin. When he was wounded, his shift was worked by other huntsmen, including his own son Marat, but Ivan

was always regarded as the most experienced, the one
to be trusted with the most responsible jobs. They tried
to take care of Ivan Popadya. Meanwhile, he and his
son studied the habits and the calls of the wild inhabi-
tants of the forest—the bears, wolves, and boars—and
improved their professional skills.

The accident happened a long time ago, when the
American politician Kissinger visited our country. He
was conducting important negotiations, and a lot depended on whether we could sign a provisional nuclear
arms limitation treaty (this was especially important, because our enemies must not be allowed to know that we
never had any nuclear arms). So Kissinger was enter-
tained at the very highest state level, and all the various
state services were involved—for instance, when it was
discovered that he liked short, plump brunettes, a quar-
tet of plump brunette swans was found to drift across
Swan Lake on the stage of the Bolshoi Theatre, under
the glinting gaze of Kissinger's horn-rimmed spectacles
up in the government box.

It was thought easier to negotiate while hunting, and
Kissinger was asked what he liked to hunt. Probably in
an attempt at subtle political witticism, he said he pre-
ferred bears, and was surprised and rather alarmed
when next morning he was actually taken hunting. On
the way he was told that two bruins had been lined up
for him.

These two were none other than the Communists Ivan
and Marat Popadya, father and son, the finest special-
service huntsmen in the reserve. The guest of honour
laid out Ivan straightaway with a well-aimed shot, just
as soon as he and Marat reared up on their hind legs

and came out of the forest, roaring; they attached the hooks to the special loops on his body and dragged it over to the car. But the American just couldn't hit Marat, even at almost point-blank range, when Marat was deliberately moving as slowly as he could, exposing the full expanse of his chest to the American's bullets. Suddenly something quite unpredictable happened—the foreign guest's gun jammed, and before anyone realised what was happening, he had thrown it down in the snow and flung himself at Marat with a knife. Of course, a real bear would have dealt very quickly with any huntsman who behaved like that, but Marat remembered the responsibility he bore. He lifted up his paws and growled, hoping to frighten the American away, but the hunter was out for blood now, and he ran up and stuck the knife into Marat's belly; the slim blade slipped between the plates of the bulletproof vest. Marat fell. And all this happened as his father looked on from where he lay a few metres away; they dragged Marat over to him, and Ivan realised that his son was still alive—he was groaning almost inaudibly. The blood he left on the snow wasn't the special liquid from his little rubber bladder—it was the real thing!

"Hold on, son!" Ivan whispered, swallowing his tears. "Hold on!"

Kissinger was beside himself with delight. He suggested to the officials accompanying him that they should all drink a toast right there, standing on top of the "teddy bears", as he called them, and they should sign the treaty on the spot. They covered Marat and Ivan with the board of honour from the wall of the forester's hut—it had their photographs on it—and made

an improvised table. For the next hour, Ivan saw nothing but fleeting glimpses of feet, and he heard nothing
but drunken speech in a foreign language and the swift
muttering of the interpreter; he was almost crushed
when the Americans danced on the table. When it grew
dark and everybody left, the treaty was signed and Marat was dead. A thin trickle of blood flowed from his
open jaws onto the blue evening snow, and a golden
Hero of the Soviet Union star glittered on his fur, where
the manager of the reserve had hung it. All night the father lay opposite his dead son, crying—and feeling no
shame for his tears.

•

I suddenly understood anew the long-lost meaning of
the words I was so fed up with seeing staring at me
every morning from the wall of the training hall: "Life
always has room for heroism." It was not just romantic
nonsense but a precise and sober statement of the fact
that our Soviet life is not the ultimate instance of reality
but only, as it were, its anteroom. I imagined it this
way: that there is no space anywhere in America, between the glaring shop window and the parked
Cadillac, for heroism, and there can be no space for it—
apart, of course, from that rare moment when a Soviet
spy passes by. But here in Russia, you can only be on
an apparently identical pavement outside an identical
shop window in a Post-War or Pre-War Period, and this
is what opens the door leading to heroism, not in the
external world, but within, in the very depths of the
soul.

"Well done," said Urchagin, when I shared my

thoughts with him, "only, be careful. The door leading to heroism certainly does open up within us, but it is in the external world that the act of heroism takes place. Don't fall into subjective idealism, or your proud flight aloft will be robbed in a single short second of all its meaning."

It was May, the peat bogs around Moscow were on fire, and a pale sultry sun hung in the smoke-veiled sky. Urchagin gave me a book to read, by a Japanese author who had been a kamikaze pilot during the Second World War, and I was astounded by the similarity between my state and the feelings he described. Just like him, I didn't think about what lay ahead of me but lived for the present day—engrossing myself in books and leaving the world completely behind as I gazed at the fiery explosions on the cinema screen (on Saturday evenings they showed us war films), even worrying seriously about my marks, which weren't too good. The word "death" existed in my life like a note reminding me of something I had to do that had been hanging on my wall for ages—I knew it was still there, but I never paused to look at it. Mitiok and I never discussed the subject, but when we were finally told it was time for us to begin practising on the actual space equipment, we glanced at each other and seemed to feel the first breath of an icy wind.

From the outside the moonwalker looked like a large laundry tank set on eight heavy tram wheels. Numerous different items protruded from its fuselage—various-shaped antennae, mechanical arms, and so forth. None

of these worked, and they were really there only for television, but they were very impressive all the same. The
lid of the moonwalker was covered with small oblique
incisions: this was not deliberate, it was simply that the
metal sheeting it was made from was the same as they
used on the floor in the metro, but then again, it made
the machine appear more mysterious.

The human psyche works in peculiar ways: it needs
details first of all. I remember when I was small I often
used to draw tanks and aeroplanes and show them to
my friends, and they always liked the drawings with
lots of lines that didn't really mean anything, so I actually began adding them on purpose. In just the same
way, the moonwalker managed to look like a very complicated and ingenious piece of equipment.

The lid hinged up to one side—it was hermetically
sealed with rubber padding and had several layers of
thermal insulation. Inside, in a space about the same
size as the turret of a tank, there was a slightly modified
sports-bike frame, with the pedals and just two gear-
wheels, one of which was neatly welded to the axle of
the rear pair of wheels. The handlebars were ordinary
semi-racers—they could turn the front wheels just
slightly via a special transmission system, but I was told
the necessity shouldn't arise. Shelves, empty for the
time being, protruded from the walls; attached to the
centre of the handlebars was a compass, and attached to
the floor was the green tin box of a radio transmitter
with a telephone receiver. Set in the wall in front of the
handlebars were the black spots of two tiny round
lenses, like the spy holes in apartment doors; through
them I could see the edges of the front wheels and a

decorative mechanical arm. On the opposite wall hung
the radio speaker, a perfectly ordinary square block of
red plastic with a black volume control: the Flight
Leader explained that in order to counter the sense of
psychological isolation from the native land, all Soviet
space vehicles received programmes broadcast from
Moscow's Beacon radio station. The large, convex external lenses were covered by blinkers above and at the
sides, so that the moonwalker had something like a
face, a crude and likeable face, like the ones they draw
on melons and robots in children's magazines.

When I first climbed inside and the lid clicked shut
over my head, I thought I would never be able to stand
being cooped up and cramped like that. I had to hang
over the bicycle frame, distributing my weight between
my hands on the handlebars, my legs braced against the
pedals, and the saddle, which didn't really support part
of my weight so much as determine the position my
body had to adopt. A cyclist bends over like that when
he's trying to get moving really fast—but at least he can
straighten up if he wants to, whereas I couldn't, because
my back and my head were practically jammed against
the lid. But then, after about two weeks of practice,
when I began to get used to it, it turned out there was
quite enough space in there to forget about feeling
cramped for hours at a time.

The round spy-hole lenses were immediately in front
of my face, but the lenses distorted everything so badly
there was no way I could tell what was outside the thin
steel wall of the hull. A small spot of the ground just in
front of the wheels and a ribbed antenna were powerfully magnified in clear focus, but everything else was

dissolved into zigzags and blobs, as though I were gazing down a long, dark corridor through tears on the
glass lenses of a gas mask.

The machine was fairly heavy, and it was hard to get
it moving—I even began to doubt whether I would be
able to power it across seventy kilometres of lunar desert. Just one turn round the yard was enough to make
me really tired; my back ached and my shoulders hurt.

Every other day now, taking turns with Mitiok, I went
up in the lift, then out into the yard, stripped down to
my vest and underpants, climbed into the moonwalker,
and strengthened the muscles in my legs by riding
round and round the yard, scattering the chickens and
occasionally running over one of them—not deliberately, of course; it was just that through the lenses there
was no way to tell a huddled chicken from a newspaper, for instance, or a leg wrapping the wind had blown
off the clothesline, and I couldn't brake fast enough, anyway. At first Urchagin drove in front of me in his
wheelchair to show me the way—through the lenses he
was a blurred grey-green blob—but gradually I got the
hang of it, so I could drive round the entire yard with
my eyes closed. All I had to do was set the handlebars
at a certain angle, and the machine went round in a
smooth circle, coming back to its starting point. Sometimes I even stopped looking through the spy holes and
just let my muscles work away, putting my head down
and thinking my own thoughts. Sometimes I remembered my childhood, sometimes I used to imagine what
the rapid approach of the final moment before eternity
would feel like. And sometimes I tried to finish off re-

ally old thoughts that resurfaced into consciousness. For instance, I thought about the question "Who am I?"

•

It was a question I often used to ask myself as a child, when I woke early in the morning and stared up at the ceiling. Later on, when I was a bit older, I began to ask it in school, but the only answer I got was that consciousness is a property of highly organised matter, according to Lenin's theory of reflection. I didn't understand what these words meant, and I remained as astonished as ever. How was it that I could see? Who was this "I" who saw? And what did it mean, to see? Did I see anything outside me, or was I simply looking at myself? And what did that mean—outside myself and inside myself? I often felt as if I were on the very threshold of the answer, but when I tried to take the final step, I suddenly lost sight of the "I" that was about to cross the threshold.

When my aunt went out to work, she often asked an old neighbour to look after me, and I used to ask her the same questions, taking real pleasure in seeing how hard it was for her to answer them.

["Inside you, Ommy, you've got a soul," she said, "and it looks out through your eyes, but it lives in your body like your hamster lives in that saucepan. And this soul is a part of God, who created all of us. And you are that soul."

"But then why did God stick me in this saucepan?" I asked.

"I don't know," said the old woman.

"And where is he?"

"Everywhere," said the old woman, gesturing with her arms.

"Then that means I'm God too?" I asked.

"No," she said. "Man isn't God. But he's made in God's image."

"And is Soviet man made in God's image too?" I asked, stumbling over the unfamiliar phrase.

"Of course," said the old woman.

"Are there many gods?" I asked.

"No. There is only one."

"Then why does it say in the handbook that there are lots of them?" I asked, nodding towards the atheist's handbook standing on my aunt's bookshelf.

"I don't know."

"Which god is best?"

The old woman gave the same answer again: "I don't know."

Then I asked: "Can I choose for myself, then?"

"You choose, Ommy." The old woman laughed, and I began riffling through the handbook, which had heaps of different gods in it. I especially liked Ra, the god the ancient Egyptians believed in thousands of years ago. Probably I liked him because he had a falcon's head, and pilots and cosmonauts and all sorts of heroes were often called falcons. I decided that if I really was made in a god's image, then it should be this one. I remember taking a large exercise book and copying the following extract into it:

In the morning Ra, illuminating the earth, sails along the heavenly Nile on the barque Manjet; *in the evening he transfers to the barque* Mesektet *and descends into the underworld, where he does battle with the forces of darkness as he sails along the nether Nile; and in the morning he reappears on the horizon.*

In ancient times, people could not know that the earth really circles the sun, said the dictionary, and so they invented this poetic myth.

Under the article in the dictionary was an old Egyptian picture showing Ra transferring from one barque to the other: two identical boats were drawn up side by side, and a girl in one was handing a girl in the other a hoop with a falcon sitting in it—that was Ra. What I liked most of all was that in among all the weird and wonderful items in the boats there were four grim five-storey houses which looked just like the ones built in the Moscow suburbs in Khrushchev's time.

From then on, although I responded to the name Omon, I always thought of myself as Ra: that was the name of the hero of the imaginary adventures I had before I fell asleep, when I closed my eyes and turned to face the wall—until the time when my dreams were affected by the usual developmental changes.

•

I wonder if anyone who sees a photograph of the moon-walker in the newspapers will imagine that inside this steel saucepan, which exists for the sole purpose of crawling seventy kilometres across the moon and then halting for eternity, there is a human being gazing out through two glass lenses? But what does it matter? Even if someone guesses the truth, he'll never know that this human being was me, Omon Ra, the faithful falcon of the Motherland, as the Flight Leader once called me, putting his arm round my shoulder and pointing through the window at a brightly glowing cloud.

Another subject that appeared in our study timetable—
"The General Theory of the Moon"—was classed as op-
tional for everyone except Mitiok and me. The classes
were given by a retired Lieutenant-Colonel of Philoso-
phy, Ivan Evseievich Kondratiev. Somehow I didn't take
to him, although I had no real reason for disliking him
and his lectures were quite interesting. I remember the
unusual way he began his first class with us—he spent
half an hour reciting various poems about the moon
from pieces of paper; eventually he became so moved
that he had to stop and wipe off his glasses. I still used
to take notes then, and what I was left with from this
class was a senseless accumulation of fragmentary quo-
tations: "Like a golden drop of honey sweetly gleams the
moon . . . Of the moon and hope and quiet glory . . .
The moon, how rich the meaning of this word for every
Russian ear . . . But the world has other regions, op-
pressed by the tormenting moon, to highest strength and
supreme courage forever out of reach . . . But in the sky,
schooled to endure all things, a senselessly distorted
disc . . . He did control the flow of thought, but only by
the moon . . . The cheerless liquid moonness . . ." And
so on for another page and a half. Then Lieutenant-

Colonel Kondratiev grew more serious and began speaking in an official singsong voice:

"Dear friends! Let us recall the historic words of Vladimir Ilyich Lenin, written in 1918 in a letter to Inessa Armand. 'Of all the planets and heavenly bodies,' Lenin wrote, 'the most important for us is the moon.' Many years have passed since then, and the world has changed in many ways, but Lenin's assessment has lost none of its acuteness and fundamental relevance: time has confirmed its correctness, and the fire of these words of Lenin's still illuminates today's page in the calendar. Indeed, the moon plays an immense role in the life of humanity. The famous Russian scientist Georgy Ivanovich Gurdjieff developed the Marxist theory of the moon during the early illegal period of his activity. According to this theory, the earth had five moons in all—this is, in fact, why the star which is the symbol of our state has five points. The fall of each of the moons has been accompanied by social upheavals and catastrophes—thus, the fourth moon, which fell to earth in 1904, and is known as the Tungus Meteorite, provoked the first Russian revolution, which was soon followed by the second. Previous moon falls led to changes in sociopolitical formations—of course, the cosmic catastrophes did not affect the level of development of the forces of production, which is determined independently of human will and consciousness, or the emanations of the planets, but they did facilitate the development of the subjective preconditions for revolution. The fall of our present moon—the fifth and final one—will usher in the absolute victory of Communism throughout the solar system. In this course we shall

study Lenin's two major works on the moon—'The
Moon and Rebellion' and 'Advice from an Outsider'.
We'll begin today with a review of bourgeois falsifica-
tions of the question—those views which assert that organic life on earth serves merely as nourishment for the
moon, as the source of emanations which it absorbs.
This is incorrect, for the goal of the existence of organic
life on earth is not to feed the moon but, as Lenin demonstrated, to build a new society, free from the exploita-
tion of men numbers one, two, and three by men
numbers four, five, six, and seven . . ."

And so on. He said a lot of other complicated things,
but what I remember most vividly is an image that
struck me as amazingly poetical: a weight hanging on a
chain makes a clock work. The moon is such a weight,
the earth is the clock, and life is the ticking of the gears
and the singing of the mechanical cuckoo.

●

We had fairly frequent medical checkups—they studied
every one of us inside and out, which was understand-
able. So when I heard that Mitiok and I had to have
what they called a "reincarnation check", I thought they
would just be testing our reflexes or measuring our
blood pressure. I didn't know what the first word
meant.

But when I was summoned downstairs and I saw the
specialist who was going to examine me, I felt an un-
controllable childish fear, which was quite out of place
in view of what the immediate future held in store
for me.

The person facing me was not a doctor with a stethoscope sticking out of the pocket of his white coat; he was an officer, a colonel—only he wasn't wearing a uniform jacket, he was dressed in a strange black robe with epaulettes. He was large and fat, with a red face that looked as though it had been scalded with hot soup. Hanging on a string round his neck were a whistle and a stopwatch, and if not for his eyes, which were like the observation slit of a heavy tank, he would have looked like a football referee. But anyway, he was pleasant enough and laughed a lot, and by the end of the conversation I felt relaxed. He spoke with me in a small office where there was nothing but a table, two chairs, a couch covered with imitation leather, and a door leading into another room. He filled up several yellowish forms, gave me a measuring glass of some bitter liquid to drink, and set a small hourglass on the table. Then he went out through the second door, telling me to follow him when all the sand had fallen through the hourglass.

I remember watching the hourglass and being amazed at how slowly the grains of sand tumbled down through the narrow glass neck, until I realised that it was because each grain had its own will, and none of them wanted to fall, because for them that was the same as dying. And at the same time they had no choice, it was inevitable. The next world and this one are just like this hourglass, I thought: when everyone alive has died in one direction, reality is inverted and they come to life again; that is, they begin to die in the opposite direction.

This made me feel sad for a while, and then I noticed that the grains of sand had stopped falling a long time ago, and I ought to go and join the colonel. I felt agitated, and at the same time strangely light and airy; I remember taking ages to walk to the door behind which he was waiting for me, although in fact it was only two or three steps away. I reached for the handle and pushed, but the door didn't open. Then I tried pulling it towards me, and suddenly noticed that I was pulling not at a door but at a blanket. I was lying in my bed, and Mitiok was sitting on the edge. I felt dizzy.

"Well? What was it like in there?" asked Mitiok. He looked oddly excited.

"What? Where?" I asked, raising myself up on one elbow and trying to think what had happened.

"At the reincarnation check," said Mitiok.

"Hang on," I said, remembering how I'd just been pulling on a door handle, "hang on . . . No. I don't remember a thing."

I felt strangely empty and lonely, as though I'd been walking through fields in autumn for a long time. This was such an unusual feeling that I forgot everything else, including even the sense of approaching death that had been constantly with me during the last few months: it was no longer so sharp now, it was simply there as the background for all my other thoughts.

"Did you sign a promise not to tell?" Mitiok asked scornfully.

"Leave me alone," I said, turning to face the wall.

"These two fat-faced warrant officers in black robes just dragged you in here," he went on, "and they said to me, 'Here, take back your Egyptian'. And your blouse is covered in puke. Can't you remember anything at all?"

"Not a thing," I answered.

"Well, wish me luck," he said. "I have to go now."

"Break a leg," I said. All I wanted to do was sleep, because it seemed to me that if I fell asleep quickly enough, I'd wake up as myself again.

I heard Mitiok close the squeaky door behind him, and then it was morning.

"Krivomazov! The Flight Leader wants you!" one of our group yelled in my ear. I didn't really wake up until after I was already dressed. Mitiok's bed was empty and undisturbed: the other guys were sitting on their beds in just their vests. I could feel the tension in the air as they glanced awkwardly at each other, and Ivan wasn't even cracking any of those stupid but very funny morning jokes of his. Something had happened, and all the way up to the Flight Leader's office on the third floor above ground I tried to figure out what it was. As I walked along with my eyes screwed up against the sunlight that pierced through the curtains—I was so unused to it—I noticed my reflection in a huge dusty mirror standing in a bend in the corridor, and I was amazed at how deathly pale my face was. I realised that my feat of heroism had really begun a long time ago.

The Flight Leader stood up to greet me and shook my hand.

"How's the training going?" he asked.

"Fine, Comrade Flight Leader," I said.

He looked into my eyes, checking me out.

"Yes, I can see it is. The reason I sent for you, Omon, is that I want you to help me. Take this tape recorder," he said, pointing to a small Japanese cassette player on the table in front of him, "and these forms and a pen,

and go to room number 329. It's free just at the moment. Have you ever transcribed a tape recording?"

"No," I replied.

"It's easy. You play a bit of the tape, write down
what you heard, and then play a bit more. If you can't
make it out the first time, you listen to it as often as you
need to."

"I understand. Permission to go?"

"Granted. No, wait. I think you'll understand why I'm
asking you to do this for me. Very soon you'll have all
sorts of questions that no one down there will answer."
As he spoke, the Flight Leader jabbed his finger towards
the floor. "I could have decided not to answer them too,
but I think it's better for you to know what's going on. I
don't want you tormenting yourself unnecessarily. But
bear in mind that neither the political instructors nor
the crew must know what you find out. What's happening now is a breach of discipline on my part. So you
see, even generals commit them sometimes."

•

Without speaking, I picked up the tape recorder from
the table, together with a few yellow forms—they were
the same as the ones I had seen the day before—and
went to room 329. The curtains on the windows were
firmly closed, and the metal chair with the leather
straps on the legs and armrests still stood in the middle
of the floor, only now there were wires leading to it
from the wall. I sat at a small writing desk in the corner, placed a ruled sheet of paper in front of me, and
switched on the tape recorder.

"Thank you, Comrade Colonel . . . It's very comfort-

able, more like an armchair really, ha-ha-ha . . . Of
course I'm nervous. It's kind of like an examination, isn't it? . . . I understand. Yes. Two *i*'s—Sviridenko . . .''

I switched off the tape recorder. It was Mitiok's voice,
but it was strange somehow, as though someone had attached a blacksmith's bellows to his vocal cords instead
of his lungs—he was speaking in a relaxed, singsong
fashion, always on the outbreath. I wound the tape back
a bit and pressed "Play". I didn't stop the tape again after that.

". . . like an examination, isn't it? . . . I understand.
Yes. Two *i*'s—Sviridenko . . . No thanks, I don't smoke.
No one in our group does, they wouldn't fit in . . . Yes,
over a year now. I can hardly believe it. As a kid I used
to dream of flying to the moon . . . Of course, of course.
That's right, only people with hearts as pure as crystal. They have to be, with all the earth spread out below . . . About who on the moon? No, I've never heard
anything about it . . . Ha-ha-ha, you're pulling my
leg . . . But your room is a bit strange—well, unusual. Is
it like this everywhere here, or just in this special section? All those skulls on the shelves, my God—lined up
just like books. And all with labels, look . . . No, I
didn't mean that. If they're on the shelves, there must
be a reason. Autopsies, some kind of archives . . . I understand. I understand. Really, now! . . . How on earth
was it saved? . . . And this here, over the eye, is that
from the ice pick? . . . Mine. There were two more
forms as well. The final check is just before blast-off.
Yes. I'm ready. But, Comrade Colonel, I gave all the details . . . Just talk about myself, since I was a child? No,

thank you, I'm quite comfortable . . . Well, if that's the
procedure. You should have headrests, like they have in
cars. The pillow could fall down if I lean forward . . .
Aha, I was just wondering why you have that mirror
on the wall. So you stand the other one on the table.
What a thick candle . . . Made of what? Ha-ha-ha,
you're joking, Comrade Colonel . . . That's incredible.
Honestly, it's the first time I've seen anything like it. I
read about it somewhere, but I've never seen it done.
Incredible. It's like a corridor. Where? Into this one?
Holy Jesus, what a lot of mirrors you have, it's like
being in a hairdresser's. Why no, what do you mean,
Comrade Colonel? . . . It's just a turn of phrase I picked
up from my grandmother. I'm a scientific atheist, otherwise I wouldn't have gone to the aviation college . . . I
remember fairly well. I didn't move to Moscow till I
was eleven—I was born in one of those small towns on
a railway line—a train goes by once in three days, and
nothing else happens. Absolutely nothing. The streets
are filthy, and the geese walk down the middle. Lots of
drunks. Everything is grey—winter, summer, it makes
no difference. Two factories, a cinema. And the park, of
course, but it's better not to stick your nose in there.
And then, you know, when there's this buzzing in the
sky, you lift up your eyes and watch. No need to explain that . . . And I was always reading books, I owe
everything that's good in me to them. My favourite, of
course, was *The Andromeda Nebula*, that really made
an impression on me. Just imagine it—an iron star . . .
And on this planet black as night—a Soviet star ship,
with a swimming pool, in the middle of a circle of blue
light, and where the light ends—a hostile life form that

fears the light and has to stay hidden in the darkness.
Some kind of medusas or other—I didn't really understand what they were—and there's this black cross—I
think that's a hint at the Church and the priests. This
black cross creeps through the darkness, and the people
are working where the blue light is, mining anameson.
And then the black cross zaps them with some weird
energy! It aimed for Erg Noor, but Niza Krit shielded
him with her breast. Afterwards our guys took their
revenge—a nuclear strike out to the horizon. They
saved Niza Krit and they caught the boss medusas and
packed them off to Moscow. And I was thinking while I
read it, What great work they do in our embassies
abroad! It's a good book. I remember another one,
too . . . There was this cave . . ."

". . ."

"No, the cave came later, and it wasn't a cave, it was
corridors. Low corridors with ceilings covered in soot
from torches. At night the warriors carried torches
while they guarded the Lord Prince. Protecting him
from the Akkadians, so they said. Actually from his
brother, of course . . . Forgive me, Lord Commander of
the North Tower, if I say what I shouldn't, but everyone
here thinks the same—all the warriors and the servants.
And even if you order my tongue to be cut out, anyone
will tell you the same thing. It was Queen Shubad her-
self who garrisoned the troops here, as protection
against Meskalamdug. Whenever he goes hunting he always rides along the southern wall, with two hundred
warriors in pointed bronze caps—why does he need
them to hunt lions? Everyone talks about it. Of course
not, Lord Commander of the North Tower, you must

have been chewing cinquefoil again! I'm Ninhursag,
priest of Arrata and carver of seals. That is, when I
grow up, I shall be a priest and a carver, I'm still a boy
as yet . . . What's that you're writing? Why, you know
me. You gave me that bridle with the bronze pendants.
Don't you remember? Why . . . Just a moment . . . I was
sitting with Namtura—you know him, his ears were cut
off—and he was teaching me how to carve a triangle.
That was the hardest shape of all for me. First you
make two deep cuts, and then you use a broad chisel to
prise it out from the third side and . . . Yes, that's right,
and then someone outside dragged open the curtain in-
solently and we looked up, and there were two warriors
standing there. Great joy! they said. Our prince is a
prince no longer, but the great king Abaraggi! He had
just departed to the deity Nanna, and so we also had to
make ready to leave. Namtura wept from happiness; he
began singing something in Akkadian and tying his
things together in a bundle. But I went straight out into
the yard, telling Namtura to gather up the chisels. By
Urshu the mighty! The warriors carrying torches made
the yard as bright as day! Why no, Lord Commander of
the North Tower, of course not. Namtura mumbles away
like that all the time . . . No, I never offered any sacri-
fices, either. Don't. I am now the Nuun of the great king
Abaraggi, it is not such a simple matter to have my ears
cut off, you need a royal decree . . . Very well, I forgive
you. Then the Lord Master of the Bolt came up to me
and said: Ninhursag, take this dagger of state bronze,
you are a man now. And he gave me a bag of barley
flour—you will prepare your food along the way, he
said. Then I looked, and saw them walking around the

yard in their bronze caps. Great Urshu! I thought. I
mean, Great Anu! Meskalamdug and Abaraggi must
have made peace . . . But then, how can you argue with
a king when his every word is Anu? Then they showed
me my chariot and I climbed up into it. There was another boy standing in it—he drove the bulls. I'd never
seen him before. All I remember is that he had beads of
turquoise, expensive beads. And a dagger in his belt—
he'd just been given one too. When I looked round at
the fortress I felt a bit sad. But then the clouds parted,
and the moon shone so brightly through the gap . . .
And I felt so relaxed and happy . . . Then they moved
aside the stone slab in the cliff wall beside the stables,
and there was the entrance to the cave. I never knew
there was a cave there. I really didn't . . . May I never
be valorous in battle! It was you there! I remember now.
And then, Lord Commander of the North Tower, you
came over to us with two bowls of beer and said it was
from the king's brother Meskalamdug. You were wearing the same skirt, but you had a painted bronze cap on
your head. We drank it down. I'd never drunk beer before. Then the other boy shouted something, and tugged
on the reins, and we set off—straight into the gap in the
cliff face. I remember the road led downwards, and
along the sides—I couldn't see, it was dark . . . Afterwards? Afterwards I found myself here in your tower.
Was it the beer that affected me like that? Will they
punish me? Intercede for me, Lord Commander of the
North Tower. Tell them what happened. Or give them
the tablets—you've written it all down. Of course I have
it . . . No, I won't give you it, I'll apply it myself. No
one gives away their own seal, by U . . . Anu the Inter-

cessor! There! Do you really like it? I made it myself. It took three attempts to get it right. This is the god Marduk. What fence? Those are the higher gods. Intercede for me, Lord Commander of the North Tower! I'll carve three seals for you. No, I'm not crying . . . There, I've stopped. Thank you. You are a man of wisdom and power. Don't tell anyone I was crying . . . They'll say, What kind of priest of Aratta is he, if a drink of beer makes him cry . . . Of course I want to. Where? To the south or the north? Your wall is entirely covered in mirrors. I understand . . . Yes, I know that. It was when Ninlil went to bathe in the clear flowing waters, and then came out onto the bank of the canal. Her mother told her again and again, but still she came out onto the bank of the canal, and Enlil put a child in her belly there. And afterwards he came to Kiur, and the council of the gods said: Enlil, violator of women, be gone from the city! And of course, Ninlil followed him . . . No, it's not too bright. The other two? That was later, when Enlil disguised himself as a watchman at the ford and Ninlil was already carrying Nanna beneath her heart . . ."

" . . . "

"But then, those two are simply different aspects of one and the same deity. You could say that Hecate is the dark and mysterious aspect, while Selene is the bright and marvellous aspect. But I must admit I'm not very knowledgeable in this area—I just heard a thing or two in Athens . . . Yes, I was. In Domitian's time. I was hiding there. Otherwise, Father Senator, you and I wouldn't be riding in this sedan chair now . . . The usual thing—*lèse majesté*. They claimed my master had

a statue of the Princeps in his courtyard, and two slaves
were buried beside it. He never had such a statue. Even
under Nerva we were afraid to go back. But there's
nothing to be afraid of with the present Princeps. He
sent Plinius Secundus himself to us as his Legate—how
the times have changed, glory be to Isis and Serapis! It's
no accident . . . Why no, what do you mean, Father
Senator, I swear by Hercules! I picked that up in Athens, the place is just packed with Egyptians . . . What
interesting tablets you have, you can hardly see the wax
at all. And the lion's muzzles—are they electron? You
don't say, Corinthian bronze . . . It's the first time I've
seen it . . . But you already know me—Sextius Rufinus.
No, I'm a freedman. A sedan chair is really a marvellous thing—if the slaves are skilful, that is—you can
write as you ride along. And the lamp burns just like in
a room, and the stone pines float past outside . . . Well
now, Father Senator, I see you can read a man's heart.
I'm constantly composing verse to myself. It's not Mar-
tial, of course, I'm just blunting styli really . . . 'I sing a
song in petty verse,/As one time Catullus did sing,/And
also Calvus and the ancients./What does it matter to
me?/I have chosen verse, quitting the forum . . .' I exag-
gerate, of course, Father Senator, but that's what poetry
is for. Actually, it was literature that made me a witness
in the trial of the Christians. I went to see our Legate. A
great man . . . Well, I wasn't exactly a witness. No, no, I
wrote down everything just the way it was—he really is
from Galilee, that Maximus. They meet at his house by
night and breathe some kind of smoke. Then he goes up
on the roof wearing nothing but his sandals and crows
like a cock—as soon as I saw it I knew they were Chris-

tians . . . I made up the bit about the bats, of course.
But what does it matter? They're bound for the gladiator
school anyway. But I really took a liking to our Legate.
Yes . . . He invited me over to his table and read my
verse. Then he said: Sextius, you must come to dinner.
At the full moon. I'll send someone for you, he said. I
gathered up all my scrolls of verse—he's bound to send
them to Rome, I thought. I put on my finest cloak . . .
No, I can't wear the toga, I'm not a Roman citizen. We
set off, but the road led out of town. We were travelling
a long time, and I fell asleep in the carriage. When I
woke up I saw a building, something between a villa
and a shrine, and torchbearers. Well, we went inside
and through into the courtyard. There was a table already laid under the open sky, and everything was lit
up by the moon—it was unbelievably huge. The slaves
said to me, The Lord Legate will be out in a minute, lie
down at the table and have some wine. This is your
place, under the marble lamb. I lay down and began to
drink, and all the others lying there kept looking at me
in silence. I wonder, I thought, what the Legate can
have told them about my verse . . . I began to feel quite
uncomfortable. But then two harps began to play behind
a screen, and suddenly I felt so happy—it was remarkable. Somehow I found myself up on my feet and dancing . . . And then tripods of fire appeared, and some
other people in yellow tunics. I think they were a little
out of their minds—they just sat there and sat there,
then suddenly they would stretch out their arms
towards the moon and start singing something in Greek
. . . No, I couldn't make it out—I was dancing and en-
joying myself. Then the Lord Legate appeared—he was

wearing a pointed Phrygian cap with a silver disc and carrying a reed pipe. His eyes were glittering. He poured me more wine. You write fine verse, Sextius, he said. Then he started talking about the moon—exactly like you, Father Senator. Heh, heh, I keep wondering what we're doing riding in this sedan chair? That's right . . . You're in your toga now, but then you were wearing a tunic and a pointed Phrygian cap, like the Legate's. Yes, and you were holding a red lance with a horse's tail. I felt awkward about turning my back to you, but the Legate kept saying to me, Look at Hecate, Sextius, and I'll play my pipe for you. He started playing—really quietly, and I looked up and went on looking, and then you started asking me about Hecate and Selene. But how did I manage to get into your se-dan chair? Is anything wrong? Well, praised be Is . . . Hercules. Apollo and Hercules . . . Very well, I'll take them back, I brought them for the Legate to read. Are you a literary man too, Father Senator? I see you keep writing all the time. Aha. A keepsake. You liked the verses too. 'This hour for you does Liei walk, and in her hair—a regal fragrant rose.' Of course. Let me apply my cameo. Never mind, the carving is quite shallow, it doesn't need much wax to print the image. Are we al-most there? Thank you, Father Senator, my hair was rather dishevelled. How much would a mirror like that cost in the metropolis? You don't say? In Bythinia we can buy a house for that sum. Is it Corinthian bronze too? Silver? And there's an inscription . . ."

". . ."

"Never mind, I can make it out. Now . . . 'To Lieuten-ant Wulf for Eastern Prussia. General Ludendorff.' Oh, I

beg your pardon, Brigadenführer, it came open by itself.
What a remarkable cigar case, it shines just like a mirror. So in 1915 you were already a lieutenant? And a
flier too? Come now, Brigadenführer, it's embarrassing.
Because of these three crosses I can't fly a single assignment. There are plenty of Yaks and MiGs, they say, but
we have only one Vögel von Richthofen. If it weren't for
this special mission, I'd probably be mouldering in an
empty barracks somewhere . . . Yes, my name is written
just like 'bird'. My mother was upset at first, when she
found out what my father wanted to call me. But then
Baldur von Schirach—he was a friend of my father's—
dedicated an entire poem to me. They study it in the
schools nowadays . . . Careful, they're shooting from
that window over there . . . Oh no, the wall's good and
thick . . . I can imagine what he would have written if
he'd known about the special mission. It was a real
poem all in itself. I believed them when they said they
were transferring me to the Western Front, and I only
just found out what was happening in Berlin. At first, of
course, I was annoyed. Have they nothing better to do
in Anenerbe, I thought, than to recall combat pilots
from the front? But when I saw the plane—Holy Virgin
Mary! Straightaway . . . Why, of course not, Brigadenführer, it's just that I lived in Italy as a child. Yes. In all
my years of flying I never saw anything so beautiful. It
took some time for me to work out what it actually was
—an Me-109 with a special engine and extended wings
. . . Damn, the magazine's jammed . . . Okay, I'll fix
it . . . Anyway, the moment I stepped into the hangar it
took my breath away. So light and white—it seemed to
glow in the darkness. But what really surprised me was

the training. I thought I'd be studying equipment, but
instead of that they used to bring me to you at Anenerbe and measure my skull, and all the time Wagner's
music was playing. If I asked any questions, no one answered. When they woke me up that night, I was sure
they were going to measure my skull again. But no,
when I looked out of the window there were two Mer-
cedes standing there with their engines running . . . Ex-
cellent shot, Brigadenführer! Right on the turret. Where
on earth did you get the knack . . . Well, we got in and
drove away. Afterwards . . . Yes, there was a cordon of
SS men with torches. We drove past them and came out
of the forest, and there was a building with columns,
and an airfield. There was no one at all around, just a
light breeze blowing and the moon in the sky. I was
sure I knew all the airfields around Berlin, but I'd never
seen this one. My plane was standing there on the run-
way, with something white hanging under the fuselage,
like a bomb, but they would not even let me stop beside
it, they brought me straight into this building . . . No, I
don't remember. All I remember is the Wagner. They
told me to get undressed and they washed me like a
child . . . No, let's keep the grenades, we'll need them
later . . . So they massaged my skin with oil—it smelt
of something ancient, a pleasant kind of smell. And
they gave me a flying suit, entirely white. With all my
decorations on the chest. Well, Vögel, I thought, this is
it . . . All my life I dreamed of something of the sort.
Then the men from Anenerbe said: Walk across to the
plane, Captain. They'll tell you everything there. They
all took turns shaking me by the hand, and I set out.
My boots were white too, I was afraid to step in the

dust . . . Just a moment . . . I went up to the plane, and there . . . Why, it was you, Brigadenführer, not in that helmet, but in a black pointed cap . . . And you started explaining everything to me—ascent to eleven thousand, set course for the moon, and press the red button on the left panel . . . Damn. Just missed one! . . . They gave me a white map case, and then coffee with cognac from a thermos flask. No thank you, I said, I don't drink before takeoff, and you said strictly: Do you know who sent that coffee, Vögel? Then I turned round and I saw him—I would never have believed it. Just like in the newsreels, even the same double-breasted jacket. But he was wearing a pointed cap and there was a pair of binoculars round his neck. And the moustache was a bit wider than it is in the portraits . . . Or perhaps the moonlight made it look like that. He waved, just like in the stadium . . . So anyway, I drank the coffee, got into the plane, put on the oxygen mask, and took off. And immediately I felt so good, my lungs felt huge. I climbed to eleven thousand and set a course for the moon—it was immense, it seemed to cover half the sky —and I looked down. Everything below looked green, and there was a river glinting . . . Then I pressed the button, and I began keeling over to the right, and I can't remember how I made a landing . . . Sign it? And you scribble something down for me as a keepsake. Thank you . . . Did many of them break through to Berlin? That's clear enough . . . It's nothing, from the crushed brick, probably. My nose isn't broken . . . Aha, I see, it's nothing at all. You could shave with a cigar case like this, and you wouldn't need a mirror . . . Thank you . . ."

"..."

"No thank you, no more. I didn't really ask for it. You put them there yourself, Comrade Colonel, when you lit the candle ... Well, what next—I read a lot of books, and then I made myself a small telescope. I looked at the moon mostly. Once I even got dressed up as a moonwalker for one of the school shows. I remember that evening very well ... All the kids were gathered in the hall in their simple costumes—they could all dance. But in my costume, if I went down on all fours, I looked just like a moonwalker. The hall was filled with music, everyone was getting red in the face ... I stood by the door and then crawled around the empty school on all fours. The corridors were dark and empty. I crawled up to a window, and outside up in the sky was the moon. It wasn't even yellow, but kind of green, like in Kuindzhi's picture—do you know it? I have it hanging above my bed, I cut it out. It was then I swore to myself I would get to the moon ... Ha-ha-ha ... If you do your best for me, Comrade Colonel, then I'm sure to get there ... What next? After school I went to the Zaraisk flying school, and then straight here ... Does that give you some idea? Yes, I know, Comrade Colonel, it's always better man to man ... Sign it? You don't mind blue ink? That's right. A simple heart, a short statement ... Yes, please. Raspberry, if possible. Where do you get the cylinders for the syphon? Oh, what a silly question ... Comrade Colonel, may I ask another question? Is it true they bring the soil from the moon to your department? I don't remember, someone in our crew ... Of course I would like to see it, I've only seen it on television ... What! How much does a jar like that hold,

about three hundred grammes? Could I? Thank you . . .
Thank you very much . . . Could you give me another
sheet, just to pack it better . . . Thank you. I remember.
To the right along the corridor to the lifts, and then
down. I won't make it? It's still affecting me? All right,
then, show me . . . What a strange pointed cap you
have. No, I like it. We had caps like that in the army
during the civil war. Very handsome, but unusual, no
peak and a round cockade . . . No, I haven't forgotten.
Left, you say? And why are you carrying that torch?
The electrician . . . I see, he needs a special pass. Light
the way for me, the steps are steep . . . just like in our
landing module. Comrade Colonel, it's a dead end . . ."

There was a click, and then the different sound of a
man and a woman singing in unison. The brightness in
their voices contrasted jarringly with what I had been
listening to.

I turned off the tape recorder—I felt terribly afraid. I
remembered the colonel in the black robe with the
whistle and the stopwatch hanging round his neck, and
I realised that no one had asked Mitiok any questions—
every time he had responded to the quiet note of the
whistle, as it interrupted his monologue.

None of the others asked me about Mitiok. He wasn't
actually friendly with anyone except me, apart from
playing a few games with homemade cards with Otto.
His bed was already gone from our box, and only the
coloured pictures from the magazines were left hanging
on the wall to remind us that a boy called Mitiok had
ever existed. In class everyone acted as though nothing
had happened; Colonel Urchagin was particularly
cheery and jolly.

Meanwhile, our small group, which seemed not to notice the loss of one of its members, carried on as usual.
No one actually said as much, but it was obvious: we
would be flying soon. The Flight Leader met with us
several times to tell us how he had fought in a partisan
detachment during the war; we had our photographs
taken—first separately, then all together, and then in
front of the banner with all the teaching staff. Above
ground we began to run into new cadets—they were being trained separately from us, and I didn't actually
know what for: there was talk of sending some automatic probe to Alpha Microcephalus immediately after
our expedition, but I was never really certain that the
new boys were the probe's crew.

One evening in early September I was unexpectedly

summoned to the Flight Leader. He wasn't in his office, and the adjutant in the anteroom, who was trying to combat his boredom with an old number of *Newsweek*, told me he was in room 329.

I could hear voices and something that sounded like laughter behind the door with the number 329. I knocked, but no one answered. I knocked again and turned the handle.

A cloud of tobacco smoke hovered just below the ceiling, reminding me somehow of that vapour trail in the air space over the Zaraisk flying school. There was a small Japanese man sitting in the metal chair in the centre of the room, his arms and legs strapped down—I knew he was Japanese from the white rectangle with a round red sun on the sleeve of his flying suit. His lips were blue and swollen, one eye was shrunk to a narrow slit in the centre of a crimson bruise, and his overalls were spattered with blood—some of the red spots were fresh, others already dried and brownish-looking. Landratov was standing in front of the chair in his tall gleaming boots, wearing the dress uniform of a lieutenant of the Air Defence Forces. Over by the window a short young man in civilian clothes was leaning against the wall with his arms crossed on his chest. The Flight Leader was sitting at the table in the corner, staring absentmindedly right through the Japanese and tapping on the table with the blunt end of a pencil.

"Comrade Flight Leader!" I began, but he stopped me with a wave of his hand and began gathering into a file the papers that were scattered about the table. I looked across at Landratov.

"Hi," he said, extending a broad palm in my direction; then, taking me completely by surprise, he punched the Japanese right in the stomach. The Japanese croaked faintly.

"The bastard doesn't want to go on a joint mission!" Landratov said, and shrugged, his eyes round with astonishment; then he turned his feet out in an unnatural fashion and performed a quick dancing squat with a double slap to his boots.

"Stop it, Landratov!" barked the Flight Leader, getting up from the table.

I heard a low whine, filled with hatred, coming from the corner of the room, and when I looked I saw a dog sitting up on its hind legs in front of a dark-blue bowl with a picture of a rocket on it. It was a very old husky, with eyes that were completely red, but more astonishing to me than its eyes was the light-green uniform jacket that covered its body, with the epaulettes of a major-general and two orders of Lenin on the chest.

"Let me introduce you," said the Flight Leader, catching my eye. "Comrade Laika. The first Soviet cosmonaut. Her parents, by the way, were colleagues of ours. They worked in the security branch too, but up in the north."

A small flask of brandy appeared in the Flight Leader's hands, and he poured some into the bowl. Laika made a feeble snap at his wrist but missed, and then she began whining again.

"She's a smart one," the Flight Leader said with a smile. "If only she wouldn't piss all over the place. Landratov, go and get a rag."

Landratov went out.

"Ioi o tenki ni narimasita ne," said the Japanese, part-

ing his lips with some difficulty. *"Hana va sakuragi, hito va fudzivara."*

The Flight Leader turned an inquiring expression to the young man by the window.

"He's delirious, Comrade Lieutenant-General," said the young man.

The Flight Leader picked up his file from the table.

"Let's go, Omon."

We went out into the corridor, and he put his arm round my shoulders. Landratov passed us with a rag in his hand, and as he closed the door of room 329 he winked at me.

"Landratov's still young," the Flight Leader said thoughtfully. "He's a bit wild. But he's a fine flier. Born to it."

We walked on a few metres in silence.

"Well now, Omon," said the Flight Leader, "you're for Baikonur the day after tomorrow. This is it."

I'd been expecting the words for months, but still it felt as if I'd been hit in the solar plexus by a snowball with a heavy metal bolt inside it.

"Your call sign, as you requested, is 'Ra'. It was hard" —the Flight Leader gestured upward significantly with his finger—"but we won out in the end. Only don't you say anything yet down there." He jabbed his finger downwards.

•

During the final test run on the model rocket I was simply a spectator—the other guys did the test while I sat on a bench by the wall and watched. I had passed my test a week earlier, up in the yard, when I rode the fully

equipped moonwalker round a figure eight a hundred
metres long in six minutes. The team's timing was spot
on, and afterwards we were lined up in front of the
rocket for a farewell photograph. I never saw it, but I
can easily imagine what it looks like: at the front is
Sema Anikin in his padded jacket, with streaks of engine oil on his hands and face; behind him, leaning on
an aluminium cane, is Ivan Grechko in his long sheepskin coat, with an oxygen mask dangling on his chest;
behind him, in a silver spacesuit padded with warm
patches of flannelette blanket decorated with yellow
ducklings, is Otto Plucis—his helmet was pushed up
and back, making it look like a hood frozen solid in the
cosmic frost. Next is Dima Matiushevich, in a spacesuit
that's exactly the same, except the blanket has plain
green stripes instead of ducklings; the last member of
the team is me, in my cadet uniform. Behind me, in his
electric-powered chair, sits Colonel Urchagin, with the
Flight Leader standing to his left.

"And now, following established tradition for these
occasions," the Flight Leader said when the photo had
been taken, "we'll go up and spend a few minutes on
Red Square."

We walked across the hall and lingered for a moment
by the small iron door—lingered for a final look at the
rocket that was an exact replica of the one on which we
would soon go soaring up into the sky. The Flight
Leader took a key from the bunch he carried and
opened a small iron door in the wall, and we set off
along a corridor which led in a direction that was new
to me.

We wove this way and that for quite a while between

stone walls festooned with wires of various colours: the
corridor made several turns, and at times the ceiling
was so low that we had to stoop. In one place I noticed
faded flowers lying in a shallow niche, and on the wall
beside it was a small memorial plaque with the words:
"On this spot in 1932 Comrade Serob Nalbandian was
villainously slain with a spade." Then a red carpet run-
ner appeared under our feet; the corridor began to
widen out and finally ended at a staircase.

The staircase was very long, and it was flanked by a
smooth incline a metre wide with narrow steps at its
centre. I realised why it was built that way when I saw
the Flight Leader pushing Colonel Urchagin's wheelchair up it. When he tired, Urchagin put on the hand
brake and they stood still for a while, so the others
didn't walk too fast, especially since long flights of
steps were difficult for Ivan to cope with. Eventually we
arrived at a pair of heavy oak doors covered with
carved emblems; the Flight Leader unlocked the doors
with another of his keys, but the doors were swollen
from dampness and opened only when I put my shoulder against them and shoved with all my strength.

The daylight was dazzling; some of us put a hand
over our eyes, others turned away, and only Colonel Urchagin sat there calmly, with the usual half-smile on his
face. When we got used to the light, it turned out we
were facing the grey headstones in front of the Kremlin
wall, and I guessed we must have come out of the back
entrance of the Lenin Mausoleum. It was so long since
I'd seen the sky over my head that I felt dizzy.

"Every single one of our Soviet cosmonauts," the
Flight Leader said softly, "has come here before their

flight, to these stones that are sacred to every Soviet citizen, in order to take a little part of this place into
space with them. Our country's labours have been hard
and long, it all began with nothing but gun carts and
machine guns, and now you young lads work with
highly complex automatic systems"—he paused and ran
a cold, unblinking gaze round all our eyes—"which
have been entrusted to you by the Motherland, and
which Bamlag Ivanovich and I have explained to you in
our lectures. I am sure that as you tread the surface of
the Motherland for the final time you will each take
with you a little part of Red Square, though just what
that particle will be for each of you, I cannot say . . ."

We stood in silence on the surface of our native
planet. It was daytime. The sky was slightly overcast,
and the sweeping branches of the blue firs swayed
gently in the wind. There was a scent of flowers. The
bells began chiming five o'clock; the Flight Leader
glanced at his watch, adjusted the hands, and said that
we still had a few minutes.

We went out onto the steps in front of the main door
of the mausoleum. There was no one at all on Red
Square, unless you counted the two sentries who had
just come on duty and gave no sign at all that they saw
us, and three sentries' backs receding in the direction of
the Spasskaya Tower. I glanced around, drinking in everything I saw and felt: the grey walls of GUM, the hollow fruit and vegetable shapes of St. Basil's Cathedral,
the Lenin Mausoleum, the green dome topped by a red
flag that I knew was behind the wall, the pediment of
the Historical Museum, and the low grey sky, which
looked as though it had turned its back on the earth and

was probably still unaware that soon it would be ripped open by the iron phallus of a Soviet rocket.

"It's time," said the Flight Leader.

The guys walked slowly back behind the mausoleum. A minute or so later only Colonel Urchagin and I were left under the word LENIN. The Flight Leader looked at his watch and coughed, but Urchagin said: "One moment, Comrade Lieutenant-General. I want to say a few words to Omon."

The Flight Leader nodded and withdrew around the polished marble corner.

"Come here, my boy," said the colonel. I went over to him. The first large, scattered raindrops were falling on the cobblestones of Red Square. Urchagin groped in the air, and I held out my hand to him. He caught it, squeezed it slightly, and tugged it towards him. I bent over, and he began to whisper in my ear. As I listened to him, I watched the steps in front of his wheelchair gradually turning darker in the rain.

Comrade Urchagin spoke to me for about two minutes, pausing at length between his words. When he stopped talking, he squeezed my hand again and let go of it.

"Now go and join the others," he said.

I took a step in the direction of the mausoleum, then turned back and asked: "What about you?"

The raindrops were falling more and more thickly.

"No matter," he said, extracting an umbrella from a holster-like case on the side of the wheelchair. "I'll ride around here for a while."

And that was what I carried away with me from Red Square that early evening: the darkened cobblestones and a thin figure in an old military jacket, sitting in an invalid chair and struggling to open a black umbrella.

Dinner was pretty bad that evening: soup with macaroni stars, skinny chicken with rice, and boiled fruit; usually when I'd drunk the liquid, I ate all the boiled fruit, but this time after I'd eaten a single bitter wrinkled pear, I began to feel sick and I pushed my plate away.

It felt as if I were riding on a pedal boat through thick reeds with huge telegraph poles sticking up out of them. The pedal boat was strange somehow, unusual, the pedals not in front of the seat but improvised from an ordinary bicycle: set between the two thick, long floats was a bicycle frame with the word "Sport" on it. I hadn't any idea where all these reeds and the pedal boat had come from, or what I was doing there. But I wasn't really bothered about it. Everything around me was so beautiful I just wanted to ride on and on and keep looking, and probably I'd have been quite happy to go on like that for ages. The sky was particularly lovely— long, narrow, lilac-coloured clouds hung above the horizon, looking like a string of strategic bombers. It was warm; I could just hear the propeller splashing in the water, and there was an echo of distant thunder from the west.

Then I realised it wasn't thunder. At regular intervals everything in me—or everything around me—was shaken, and my head began to buzz. With every successive blow all my surroundings—the river, the reeds, the sky over my head—seemed to fade a little more. The world was becoming as familiar in its finest details as the door of the bathroom at home seen from the inside, and it was all happening very quickly, until I noticed that the bicycle was no longer on water or surrounded by reeds but inside a transparent sphere that separated me from everything around me. Every blow made the wall of the sphere thicker and more solid; it let through less and less light, until finally there was total darkness. Then the sky over my head was replaced by a ceiling, a feeble glow of electric light appeared, and the walls began to change their shape, closing in on me and bending out to form shelves stacked with glasses, cans, and other stuff. And then the rhythmical shuddering of the world became what it had been from the very start—a telephone ringing.

I was sitting on the saddle inside the moonwalker, clutching the handlebars and leaning right down over the frame; I was dressed in a padded jacket, a fur cap with earflaps, and fur boots; an oxygen mask hung round my neck like a scarf. The ringing came from the green box of the radio screwed to the floor. I picked up the receiver.

"Why, you fucking useless shithead!" a monstrous bass voice boomed in my ear in a tone of anguished suffering. "What're you doing in there, wanking?"

"Who's that?"

"Head of Central Flight Control Colonel Khalmuradov. Are you awake?"

"What?"

"Fuck you, that's what. Make ready, one minute to launch!"

"Ready in one minute, sir!" I muttered in reply, biting my lip in horror and grasping for the wheel with my free hand.

"You asshole," the receiver hissed indistinctly and began croaking—the man yelling at me was obviously holding the receiver away from his face while he talked to someone else. Then there was a ping in the phone, and I heard a different voice, mechanical and impersonal, but with a strong Ukrainian accent:

"Fifty-nine . . . fifty-ate . . ."

I was in that state of shame and shock that makes a man groan out loud or scream obscenities; the thought that I'd almost made an irrevocable mistake obscured everything else. As I followed the numbers exploding in my ears, I tried to remember what had happened and realised I probably hadn't really done anything all that terrible. All I could remember was lowering the glass of boiled fruit from my mouth and getting up from the table after I suddenly lost my appetite. The next thing I knew, the phone was ringing and I had to answer it.

"Tirty-tree . . ."

I noticed the moonwalker was fully equipped. The shelves that had always been empty before were densely stacked—on the bottom shelf there were cans of Great Wall Chinese corned beef, covered in gleaming Vaseline; on the upper shelf there was a map case, a mug, a can opener, and a pistol in a holster, everything secured by wire. Resting against my left hip was an oxygen cylinder with the word "Inflammable" on it, and against my right hip an aluminium milk churn that reflected the light of the small electric lamp glowing on the wall. Under the lamp hung a map of the moon marked with two black circles: under the lower circle were written the words "Landing Site". Hanging beside the map on a piece of string was a red marker pen.

"Sax-teen . . ."

Beyond the two spy holes there was total darkness—
which was what I should have expected, I realised,
since the moonwalker was covered by the rocket's nose
cone.

"Nine . . . Ate . . ."

I recalled Comrade Urchagin's words: "Those final
seconds of the countdown, what are they but the voice
of history speaking through millions of television
screens."

"Tree . . . Two . . . Win . . . Blastoff."

Somewhere far below me I heard a rumbling and
roaring that grew louder with every second, until soon
it was beyond all imagining, as though hundreds of
sledgehammers were pounding on the rocket's iron fuselage. Then the shuddering began, and I banged my
head against the wall in front of me a few times—if not
for the fur cap,·I'd probably have beaten my brains out.
A few cans of corned beef fell to the floor, then everything suddenly keeled over so sharply I thought for a
second we were going to crash—and the next moment
there was a distant voice in the telephone receiver that I
was still pressing to my ear:

"Omon! You're flying!"

"We're off," I remembered my instructions and
yelled, just as Gagarin did when he was first catapulted
out into space.

The roaring became a steady, powerful rumbling,
while the shuddering became the kind of vibration you
feel in a train when it's already picked up speed. I put
the receiver back on the hook, and the phone immediately rang again.

"Omon, are you all right?"

It was Sema Anikin's voice, speaking over a monotonous recitation of information about the first section of the flight.

"I'm fine," I said. "But why are we . . . Ah, I see . . ."

"We thought they'd have to postpone the launch, you were so sound asleep. The moment's calculated to the split second. The entire trajectory depends on it. They even sent a soldier up the gantry and he kicked the nose cone to wake you up. They were trying to call you on the radio for ages."

"Aha."

We said nothing for a few seconds.

"Listen," Sema began again, "I've only got four minutes left, not even that. Then I have to detach the first stage. We've all said goodbye to each other, except for you . . . This is our last chance to talk."

I couldn't think of the right words to say, and all I felt was embarrassment and weariness.

"Omon!" Sema called me again.

"Yes, Sema," I said, "I hear you. We're flying, d'you understand?"

"Yes," he said.

"How are you feeling?" I asked, realising just how senseless and insulting the question was.

"I'm okay. How about you?"

"Me too. What can you see?"

"Nothing. There's no way to see out. The noise is terrible. And the shaking."

"Up here too," I said, then stopped.

"Okay," said Sema, "my time's up. You know what? Think about me when you land on the moon, okay?"

"Of course," I said.

"Just remember there was a guy called Sema. The first stage. Promise?"

"I promise."

"You've got to get there and finish the job, you hear me?"

"Yes."

"Time's up. Goodbye."

"Goodbye, Sema."

There were several hollow knocks in the receiver, and then through the crackle of interference I heard Sema's voice loud and clear as he sang his favourite song.

"O-oh, in Africa there's a river as long as this . . . O-oh, in Africa there's a mountain as high as this . . . O-oh, crocodiles and hippos . . . O-oh, monkeys and rhinos . . . O-oh . . . Ah-ah-ah-ah . . ."

On the word "rhinos" there was a crackling like a piece of tarpaulin ripping, and a moment later there were just short beeps, but just a second before that—if it wasn't my imagination—Sema's song turned into a scream. I was jolted again, my back hit against the ceiling, and I dropped the receiver. From the change in the roaring of the engines, I guessed the second stage had begun firing. Probably the most terrible thing for Sema was switching on the engine. I imagined what it was like—breaking the safety glass and pressing the red button, knowing all the while that a second later the huge gaping openings of the rocket tubes would spring into violent life. Then I remembered Ivan, and I grabbed the receiver again, but it was still beeping.

I hit the hook a few times and yelled: "Ivan! Ivan! Can you hear me?"

"What is it?" I finally heard him say.

"Sema, he's . . ."

"Yes," he said, "I heard it all."

"Are you going soon?"

"In seven minutes," he said. "D'you know what I'm thinking about now?"

"What?"

"I suddenly remembered how I used to catch pigeons as a kid. You know, we took this big wooden crate and sprinkled breadcrumbs under it and stood it on edge, and we propped up the opposite edge with a stick with about ten metres of string tied to it. Then we hid in the bushes or behind a bench, and when a pigeon wandered under the crate, we pulled the string. Then the crate fell on it."

"That's right," I said. "We did the same."

"And you remember, when the crate comes down, the pigeon starts trying to fly off and beats its wings against the sides, so the crate even jumps about?"

"I remember," I said.

Ivan didn't say anything else.

In the meantime, it had turned quite cold. And it was harder to breathe too—after every movement I wanted to catch my breath, as if I'd just run up a long flight of stairs. I began lifting the oxygen mask to my face to take a breath.

"And I remember how we used to make bombs with cartridge cases and the sulphur from matches. You stuff it in real tight, and there has to be a little hole in the side, and you put several matches in a row beside it . . ."

"Cosmonaut Grechka." The bass voice in the receiver

was the one that had woken me with abuse before the start of the flight. "Make ready."

"Yes, sir," Ivan answered without enthusiasm. "And then you tie them on with thread—insulating tape's better, because sometimes the thread comes loose. If you want to throw it out of the window, say from the seventh floor, so it explodes in midair, then you need four matches. And . . ."

"Stop that talking," said the bass voice. "Put on your oxygen mask."

"Yes, sir. You don't strike the last one with the box, though, the best thing is to light it with a dog-end. Or else you might shift them away from the hole."

I heard nothing after that except the usual crackle of interference. Then I was bounced against the wall again, and the short beeps sounded in the receiver. The third stage had fired. The fact that my friend Ivan had just departed this life at an altitude of forty-five kilometres —as simply and unpretentiously as he did everything— strangely failed to make any impression on me. I didn't feel any grief; quite the opposite, I felt a strange exhilaration and euphoria.

I suddenly realised that I was losing consciousness. That is, I didn't notice when I lost consciousness, I noticed when I regained it. A moment before, I was holding the receiver to my ear, and now it was lying on the floor; there was a ringing in my ears, and I gazed down at it in stupefaction from my saddle up under the ceiling. A moment before, the oxygen mask was hanging round my neck like a scarf—and now as I shook my head in an effort to rouse myself, it was lying on the floor beside the telephone receiver. I realised I needed oxygen, so I reached for the mask and put it to my mouth—I felt better instantly, and I could feel I was very cold. Fastening all the buttons of my padded jacket, I put the collar up and lowered the earflaps of my fur cap. The rocket was shaking slightly. I wanted to sleep, and even though I knew it wasn't a good idea, I couldn't fight it—I folded my hands on the handlebars and closed my eyes.

I dreamed of the moon—the way Mitiok used to draw it in our childhood: a black sky, pale yellow craters, and a distant mountain range. Walking slowly and smoothly towards the blazing orb of the sun hanging above the horizon was a bear, with its front paws held out in front of its muzzle: it had the golden star of a Hero of the Soviet Union on its chest, and a trickle of dried blood ran from the corner of its mouth, which was set in a pitiful grin. Suddenly it stopped and turned its face towards me. I felt it watching me, and I raised my head to glance into its motionless blue eyes.

"I and this entire world are nothing but a thought someone is thinking," the bear said in a quiet voice.

I woke up. Everything was very quiet. Clearly some part of my consciousness had maintained contact with the outside world, and the sudden silence had affected me like an alarm clock going off. I leaned down to the spy holes in the wall. The nose cone had already separated from the rocket, and there in front of my eyes was the earth.

I tried to work out how long I'd been asleep, but I couldn't put any definite figure on it. It must have been a few hours at least: I felt hungry already, and I began rummaging through the things on the upper shelf—I thought I'd seen a can opener there, but it wasn't there now. I decided it must have been shaken off onto the floor and started looking around for it, but just at that moment the phone rang.

"Hello!"

"Stand by, Ra. Omon, can you hear me?"

"Yes, Comrade Flight Leader."

"So far everything seems to be going okay. There was just one difficult moment, when the telemetry malfunctioned. Not that it actually malfunctioned, you understand, they simply activated another system in parallel and the telemetry failed to operate. They even lost control for a few minutes. That was when you were short of air, remember?"

He was speaking in a strange way, quick and excited. I decided he must be feeling very nervous, though just for a moment I suspected he was drunk.

"You gave everyone a good scare, Omon. Sleeping like that. We almost had to postpone the launch."

"I'm sorry, Comrade Flight Leader."

"Never mind, never mind. It's not your fault. They just drugged you too heavily before the trip to Baikonur. So far everything's going just fine."

"Where am I now?"

"On the working trajectory already. You're flying towards the moon. You mean you slept through the escape from earth orbit too?"

"I must have. You mean Otto's already . . ."

"Yes, Otto's gone already. Surely you can see the nose cone's already separated? But you had to do two extra orbits. Otto panicked at first. He just wouldn't switch on the rockets. We thought he'd chickened out,

but then the lad pulled himself together . . . Anyway,
he sent you his regards."

"And Dima?"

"What about Dima? Dima's okay. The automatic landing system isn't used during the inertial section of the
flight. Though he still has the corrections to make . . .
Matiushevich, can you hear us?"

"Yes, sir," said Dima's voice in the receiver.

"Okay, you rest for now," said the Flight Leader.
"Standby tomorrow at 1500 hours, then correction of
trajectory. Over and out."

I put down the receiver and pressed my eyes against
the spy holes to gaze at the blue semicircle of the earth.
I'd often read how all the cosmonauts were astounded
by the sight of our planet from space. They wrote about
some fabulously beautiful misty effect, and how the cit-
ies with their shining electric lights on the dark side reminded them of huge bonfires, and how they could
even see the rivers on the daylight side—well, none of
it's true. The thing the earth seen from space resembles
most is a large school globe, like I remembered seeing
through the steamed-up glass of a gas mask. I was soon
sick of the sight; I rested my head as comfortably as I
could on my arms and went to sleep again.

When I woke up, the earth was no longer visible. All
I could make out through the spy holes were the white
spots of the distant and unattainable stars, blurred by
the lenses. I imagined the existence of a huge, immensely hot sphere hanging entirely unsupported in the
icy void, billions of kilometres from the closest stars,
those tiny gleaming dots, of which all we know is that
they exist, and even that's not certain, because a star

can die, while its light will carry on travelling out in all
directions, so really we don't know anything about
stars, except that their life is terrible and senseless,
since all their movements through space are predeter-
mined and subject to the laws of mechanics, which
leave no hope at all for any chance encounters. But
then, I thought, even though we human beings always
seem to be meeting each other, and laughing, and slap-
ping each other on the shoulder, and saying goodbye,
there's still a certain special dimension into which our
consciousness sometimes takes a frightened peep, a dimension in which we also hang quite motionless in a
void where there's no up or down, no yesterday or tomorrow, no hope of drawing closer to each other or
even exercising our will and changing our fate; we
judge what happens to others from the deceptive twin-
kling light that reaches us, and we spend all our lives
journeying towards what we call the light, although its
source may have ceased to exist long ago. And me, I
thought, all my life I've been journeying towards the
moment when I would soar up over the crowds of what
the slogans called the workers and the peasants, the sol-
diers and the intelligentsia, and now here I am hanging
in brilliant blackness on the invisible threads of fate
and trajectory—and now I see that becoming a heavenly
body is not much different from serving a life sentence
in a prison carriage that travels round and round a cir-
cular railway line without ever stopping.

We travelled through space at a speed of two and a half kilometres a second, and the inertial section of the flight lasted about three days, but I had the feeling I'd been flying for at least a week. Probably because the sun passed in front of the spy holes several times a day, and every time I was able to watch a quite incredibly beautiful sunrise and sunset.

All that was left now of the immense rocket was the lunar module, made up of the correction and braking stage, where Dima Matiushevich was sitting, and the descent vehicle, that is, the moonwalker on its platform. In order to save fuel, the nose cone had separated before escape from earth orbit, and now there was open space beyond the fuselage of the moonwalker. The lunar module was flying backwards, so to speak, with its main rocket pointing towards the moon, and gradually the way I felt about it changed just as it had with the cool lift in the Lubyanka building, when it was transformed from a mechanism for going down underground into a device for going up to the surface.

At first the lunar module rose higher and higher above the earth, until at some point it gradually became clear that it was falling towards the moon. But there was a difference. In the lift I went down and came up with my head pointing upwards, but I hurtled out of earth orbit with my head pointing downwards; it was only later, after a day or so of the flight, that I found myself with my head upwards, falling with ever-increasing speed down a black well, clutching the handlebars of my bicycle and waiting for its nonexistent wheels to collide silently with the moon.

I had time for all these thoughts because for the time being I had nothing to do. I often felt like talking to Dima, but he was always busy with all his complicated corrections to the trajectory. Sometimes I picked up the receiver and heard his incomprehensible exchanges with the engineers at Central Flight Control:

"Forty-three degrees . . . Fifty-seven . . . Yaw . . ."

I listened to all this for a little while, then gave up on it. As far as I could understand, Dima's main task was to catch the sun in one optical device, the moon in another, measure something, and transmit the result to earth, where they had to check the actual trajectory with the projected one and calculate the length of the corrective impulse required from the engines. Judging from the fact that I was jerked about quite roughly on my saddle several times, Dima seemed to be coping with his task.

When the shocks stopped, I waited about half an hour, picked up the receiver, and called him.

"Hello! Dima!"

"Yes, I hear you," he said in his usual dry manner.

"Have you corrected the trajectory, then?"

"Seems like it."

"Was it difficult?"

"It was fine," he answered.

"Listen," I said, "where did you pick up all that stuff? All those degrees and things? We didn't have any of that in class."

"I served two years in a strategic rocket detachment," he said. "The directional system's much the same, only you use the stars. And without any radio communications—you work it all out yourself on a calculator. Make a mistake and you're fucked."

"And if you don't make a mistake?"

Dima didn't answer that one.

"What were your duties?"

"Operational officer. Then strategic officer."

"What does that mean?"

"Nothing complicated. If you're sitting in a tactical operations rocket, you're an operational officer. If you're in a strategic rocket, then you're a strategic officer."

"Is it tough?"

"It's okay. Like working as a watchman back in the everyday world. Twenty-four hours' duty in the rocket and three days off."

"So that's what turned your hair grey . . . I suppose all of you are grey."

Dima didn't answer that one either.

"It's the responsibility, is it?"

"No. More likely the training flights."

"What training flights? Ah—that's when they write in fine print on the back page of *Izvestya* that it's forbidden to sail into such and such a sector of the Pacific Ocean, is that it?"

"That's it."

"And do they have training flights often?"

"It depends, but you pull a straw every month.

Twelve times a year, the entire squadron. All twenty-four of you. That's what turns the guys' hair grey."

"And what if you don't want to pull a straw?"

"Pulling a straw is just an expression of speech. What actually happens before the training flight is the assistant political instructor goes round and gives everyone an envelope. Your straw's already in it."

"And if you get a short straw, can you refuse?"

"In the first place, it's a long straw, not a short one. And in the second place, no. All you can do is write an application for a cosmonauts' detachment. But you have to be really lucky."

"Are many people lucky?"

"I've never counted them. I was lucky."

Dima answered my questions reluctantly, with lots of rather impolite pauses. I couldn't think of anything else to ask, so I put down the receiver.

I made my next attempt to talk to him when there were only a few minutes left to braking. I'm ashamed to admit it, but I was overcome by a callous curiosity—would Dima change before . . . ? I wanted to check whether he would be as taciturn as he was during our last conversation, or whether the approaching end of his flight would make him a bit more talkative. I picked up the receiver and called him.

"Dima! This is Omon. Pick up the phone."

The answer I got was: "Listen, ring me back in two minutes! If your radio's working, switch it on now!"

Dima hung up. His voice sounded excited, and I thought they must be talking about us on the radio. But Radio Beacon was broadcasting music—when I switched on, I caught just the fading tinkle of a synthesiser; the programme was about to end, and after a few seconds there was a silent pause. Then came the time signal, and I learned that in a place called Moscow it was two in the afternoon. I waited a bit and then picked up the receiver.

"Did you hear it?" Dima asked excitedly.

"Yes," I said, "but only the very end."

"But did you recognise it?"

"No," I said.

"It was Pink Floyd. 'One of These Days'."

"How come the workers requested that?" I asked in astonishment.

"They didn't, of course," said Dima. "It's the theme tune for the programme *Life of Science*. From the album *Meddle*. Pure underground."

"You mean you like Pink Floyd?"

"Me? I'm a fan. I had all their albums. What d'you think of them?"

It was the first time I had heard Dima speak with such enthusiasm.

"Not bad in general," I said. "But not all their stuff. They have this album with a cow on the cover."

"Atom Heart Mother," said Dima.

"I like that one. And there's another one I remember —a double album with them sitting in a yard, and on the wall is a picture of the same yard with them sitting in it . . ."

"Ummagumma."

"Maybe. I don't think that's music at all."

"That's right! It's not music, it's shit!" a bass voice roared in the receiver, and we said nothing for a few seconds.

"You're wrong," said Dima when he finally spoke. "At the end there's a new version of 'Saucerful of Secrets'. A different timbre from on *Nice Pair*. Different singer, too."

I'd forgotten that.

"What do you like on *Atom Heart Mother*?" asked Dima.

"There are a couple of songs on side two. One's quiet, just a guitar, and the other has an orchestra. The ending's beautiful—tam ta-ta ta-ta ta-ta ta-ta tam-taram tra-ta-ta . . ."

"I know it," said Dima. " 'Summer '68. And the quiet song's 'If'."

"Maybe," I said. "So what's your favourite record?"

"I don't have a favourite record," Dima said haughtily. "It's not records I like, it's music. On *Meddle*, for instance, I like the first song. About the echo. It makes me cry every time I listen to it. I translated it with a dictionary. 'Overhead the Albatross pa-ra-ram, pa-ram . . . And help me understand the best I can . . .' "

Dima swallowed and fell silent.

"Your English is very good," I said.

"Yes, that's what they told me in the rocket division. The assistant political instructor said so. But that's not the point. There was one record I didn't manage to find. During my last leave I went to Moscow specially, took four hundred roubles with me. I asked around everywhere, no one had even heard of it."

"What record was that?"

"You wouldn't know it. Music from a film. It's called *Zabriskie Point*."

"Ah," I said, "I did have that one. Not the record, I

had it on tape. Nothing special really . . . Dima, why have you gone all quiet? Hey, Dima!"

The receiver crackled for a long time before Dima asked: "What's it like?"

"How can I put it?" I said. "Have you heard 'More'?"

"Sure."

"It's kind of like that. Only they don't sing. An ordinary kind of soundtrack. If you've heard 'More', you can reckon you've heard it. Typical Pinky—saxophone, synthesiser. The second side . . ."

There was a beep in the phone, and my skull cavity was filled with Khalmuradov's loud roar: "Ra, come in! What are you fucking chattering about up there? Haven't you got anything to do? Prepare the automatic system for soft landing!"

"The automatic system's ready!" Dima replied, reluctantly.

"Then commence orientation of the braking motor axis to the lunar vertical!"

"All right."

I glanced out into space through the moonwalker's spy holes and saw the moon right up close. The picture that met my eyes would have been just like the Ukrainian flag, if its top half were blue instead of black. The phone rang. I picked it up, but it was Khalmuradov again.

"Attention! At the count of three, activate the braking motor on the command of the radioaltimeter!"

"Read you," replied Dima.

"One . . . two . . ."

I hung up quickly.

The motor fired. It worked intermittently, and about

twenty minutes later my shoulder was suddenly thrown against the wall, then my back was bounced against the ceiling, and then an intolerably loud crash shook everything; I realised that Dima had passed on to immortality without saying goodbye. But I wasn't offended—apart from our final conversation he'd always been taciturn and unsociable, and I had a feeling that sitting for days at a time in the gondola of his intercontinental ballistic missile, he'd understood something which meant he never needed to say hello or goodbye again.

·

I didn't notice the landing. The shuddering and rumbling suddenly stopped, and looking out through the spy holes, I saw the same pitch blackness I had seen before the start of the flight. At first I thought something had gone wrong, then I remembered that according to plan I was supposed to land during the lunar night.

I waited for a while, not knowing what I was waiting for. Suddenly the phone rang.

"Khalmuradov here," said the voice. "Is everything in order?"

"Yes, sir, Comrade Colonel."

"The telemetry will be activated in a moment, and the guiderails will be lowered," he said. "You will proceed down onto the surface and report. But use the brakes, you understand?"

Then in a quieter voice, holding the receiver away from his face, he added: "Hun-der-ground. What a bastard."

The moonwalker swayed and I heard a dull thud from outside.

"Proceed," said Khalmuradov.

This was probably the most difficult part of my assignment—I had to drive down out of the descent module along two narrow guiderails lowered onto the lunar surface. The guiderails had special slots to accommodate the flanges on the moonwalker's wheels, so it was impossible to slide off them, but there was still the danger that one of the guiderails might land on a boulder, and then the moonwalker might tilt and overturn on its way down to the ground. I turned the pedals a few times and felt the massive machine lean forward and begin to move under its own momentum. I pressed the brake, but the force of inertia was too strong, and the moonwalker was dragged downwards; suddenly there was a clanging sound, the brake went slack, and my feet turned the pedals backwards several times with terrifying speed. The moonwalker rolled forward irresistibly, swayed, and came to a halt, standing evenly on all eight wheels.

I was on the moon. But I had no feelings about the fact at all; I was wondering how to put back the chain that had slipped off the cog wheel. Just when I had finally managed it, the phone rang. It was the Flight Leader. His voice sounded solemn and official.

"Comrade Krivomazov! On behalf of the entire aviation officers' corps present here at Central Flight Control, I congratulate you on the soft landing of the Soviet automated space station Luna-17B on the moon!"

I heard popping sounds, and I realised they were opening champagne. There was music too—some kind of march; I could hardly hear it, it was almost drowned out by the crackling in the receiver.

My youthful dreams of the future were born from the
gentle sadness of those evenings, far removed from the
rest of life, when you lie in the grass beside the remains
of someone else's campfire, with your bicycle beside
you, watching the purple stripes left in the western sky
by the sun that has just set, and you can see the first
stars in the east.

I hadn't seen or experienced very much, but I liked
lots of things, and I thought that a flight to the moon
would take in and make up for all the things I had
passed by, in hopes of catching up with them later; how
could I know that you only ever see the best things in
life out of the corner of your eye? As a kid I often imagined the landscapes of other worlds—rocky plains
flooded with dead light and pitted with craters; distant,
sharp-pointed mountains; a black sky with the huge
brand of a sun blazing on it amid the glittering stars. I
imagined metre-thick layers of cosmic dust, I imagined
boulders lying motionless on the surface of the moon
for billions of years—for some reason I was really excited by the idea that a boulder could lie in the same
place without moving for so long until one day I bent
down and picked it up between the thick fingers of my
spacesuit glove. I thought about how I would raise my

head to see the blue sphere of the earth, and this supreme moment of my life would link me with all the
moments when I felt I was standing on the threshold of
something wonderful beyond comprehension.

In fact, the moon proved to be a narrow, black, stuffy
space where the faint electric light came on only rarely;
it turned out to be constant darkness seen through the
useless lenses of the spy holes, and restless, uncomfortable sleep in a cramped position with my head resting
on my arms, which lay on the handlebars.

I travelled slowly, about five kilometres a day, and I
hadn't the slightest idea what the world around me
looked like. But then, of course, this kingdom of eternal
darkness probably didn't look like anything—apart from
me, there wasn't anybody for whom it could look like
anything, and I didn't switch on the headlight, in order
to save the battery. The surface of the ground beneath
me was obviously even and the machine moved
smoothly over it. I couldn't turn the handlebars at all—
they must have jammed on landing—so all I had to do
was keep turning the pedals. But my journey into space
had been so long that I refused to allow gloomy
thoughts to get me down, and I even managed to feel
happy.

Hours and days went by. When I halted, it was only
to lower my head onto the handlebars and sleep. It was
so horribly uncomfortable to use the toilet that I pre-
ferred to wait till the final moment, the way I used to
during quiet hour in kindergarten. The corned beef was
gradually running out, there was less and less water in
the milk can; every evening I extended the red line on
the map in front of me by another centimetre, and it

crept closer and closer to the small black circle where it was supposed to come to a stop. The circle was like the symbol for a metro station; it irritated me that it had no name, and I wrote one beside it—"Zabriskie Point".

.

With my right hand squeezing the nickel-plated knob in the pocket of my padded jacket, I had been staring for an hour at the label of one of the cans, with its words "Great Wall". I was having visions of warm winds over the fields of distant China, and I wasn't really interested in the tedious ringing of the phone on the floor, but I picked it up after a while.

"Ra, come in! Why don't you answer? Why aren't we moving? I can see everything here with the telemetry."

"I'm having a rest, Comrade Flight Leader."

"Report the reading on the gauge!"

I glanced at the figures in the opening in the small steel cylinder.

"Thirty-two kilometres, seven hundred metres."

"Now put out the light and listen. Looking at the map here, we can see you're very close."

I felt my heart sink, although I knew there was still a long way to go to that small black circle that gazed at me from the map like the barrel of a gun.

"To what?"

"The landing module of Luna-17B."

"But I'm Luna-17B," I said.

"Never mind, so were they."

It seemed he was drunk again. But I understood what he was talking about. It was the expedition to obtain samples of the lunar soil: that time two cosmonauts had

landed on the moon, Pasiuk Drach and Zurab Prats-
vania. They had a small rocket with them which they
used to send five hundred grammes of soil back to
earth; after that they lived on the lunar surface for one
and a half minutes, and then shot themselves.

"Careful, Omon!" said the Flight Leader. "Be cautious
now. Reduce speed and switch on the headlights."

I flicked a switch and pressed my eyes to the black
lenses of the spy holes. The optical distortion drew the
blackness around the moonwalker into an arch that
stretched out ahead of me in an endless tunnel. All I
could make out clearly was a small section of the
rough, uneven rocky surface—it was evidently ancient
basalt; every one and a half metres or so there were
long, low outcrops perpendicular to my line of movement; they reminded me of sandhills in the desert. The
strange thing was, I didn't feel them at all as I moved
along.

"Well?" asked the voice in the receiver.

"I don't see anything," I said.

"Turn off the headlights and proceed. Don't hurry."

I went on for another forty minutes. Then the moonwalker collided with something. I picked up the phone.

"Earth, come in. There's something here."

"Switch on the headlights."

Right in the centre of my field of vision lay two
hands in black leather gloves. The extended fingers of
the right hand lay over the handle of a small shovel
which still held a little sand mixed with small stones,
and the left hand gripped a Makarov pistol that gleamed
dully. There was something dark between the hands.
Looking closer, I could make out the raised collar of an

officer's padded jacket with the top of a fur cap protruding above it; the man's shoulder and part of his head
were concealed by the wheel of the moonwalker.

"What is it, Omon?" the receiver breathed in my ear.

I described briefly what I could see.

"What about the epaulettes, can you see them?"

"No, I can't."

"Move back half a metre."

"The moonwalker doesn't travel backwards," I said.
"It has pedal braking."

"Damn . . . I told the chief designer," mumbled the
Flight Leader. "I wonder who it is, Zura or Pasha. Zura
was a captain, and Pasha was a major. Okay, switch off
the headlights, you'll flatten the batteries."

"Yes, sir," I said, but before I carried out the order, I
took another look at the motionless hand and the fabric
top of the fur cap. I couldn't get moving for a while, but
then I gritted my teeth and put all my weight on the
pedal. The moonwalker jerked upwards and then, a second later, back down again.

"Proceed," said Khalmuradov, who had replaced the
Flight Leader on the phone. "You're falling behind
schedule."

•

I saved energy by spending almost all the time in total
darkness, frenziedly turning the pedals and switching
on the light for only a few seconds at a time in order to
check the compass, although this was quite pointless,
since the handlebars were useless anyway. But they ordered me to do it. It's hard to describe the sensation:
darkness, a hot, cramped space, sweat dripping from

your brow, a gentle swaying—perhaps an embryo expe-
riences something of the sort in its mother's womb.

I was aware that I was on the moon, but the immense
distance separating me from the earth was a pure ab-
straction for me. I felt as though the people I spoke with
on the phone were somewhere close by—not because I
could hear their voices clearly in the receiver, but because I couldn't imagine how the entirely immaterial official relationships and personal feelings that linked us
together could be stretched so far. But the strangest
thing was that the memories connecting me with childhood could extend over such an incomprehensible distance too.

•

When I was in school, I used to spend the summers in a
village outside Moscow. It stood on the edge of a main
highway, and I spent most of my time on the saddle of
my bike, sometimes riding up to thirty or forty kilometres a day. The bicycle wasn't very well adjusted—the
handlebars were too low, and I really had to bend down
to them—like in the moonwalker. And now, probably
because my body had been set in that pose for such a
long time, I began having light hallucinations. I seemed
to drift off into a waking sleep—in the darkness it was
particularly easy—and I dreamed I could see my
shadow on the asphalt rushing past below me, and the
white dotted line in the middle of the highway, and I
was breathing air smelling of diesel fumes. I began to
think I could hear the roar of lorries rushing past and
the hissing of tyres on asphalt, and only the next radio
contact brought me back to my senses. But afterwards I

dropped out of lunar reality and again was transported back to the Moscow highway, and I realised how much the hours I spent there had meant to me.

On one occasion Comrade Kondratiev came on the radio to talk to me and began declaiming poetry about the moon. I was wondering how to ask him to stop without being offensive, when he began reading a poem that I recognised from the very first lines as a photographic image of my soul:

Life's vital bonds we took for lasting truth,
But as I turn my head to glance at you,
How strangely changed you are, my early youth,
Your colours are not mine, and not one line is true.
And in my mind, moonglow is what I see
Between us two, the drowning man and shallow place;
Your semi-racer bears you off from me
Along the miles towards the moon's bright face,
How long now since . . .

I gave a quiet sob, and Comrade Kondratiev immediately stopped.

"What comes next?" I asked.

"I've forgotten," said Comrade Kondratiev. "It's gone clean out of my head."

I didn't believe him, but I knew it was pointless to argue or plead.

"What are you thinking about now?" he asked.

"Nothing really," I said.

"Nobody thinks of nothing," he said. "There's always some thought or other running round your head. Tell me, I'd like to know."

"Well, I often remember my childhood," I said reluctantly. "How I used to go riding on my bike. It was a lot like this. And to this day I don't understand it—there I was, riding along on my bike, with the handlebars way down low, and it was really bright up ahead, and the wind was so fresh . . ."

I stopped speaking.

"Well? What is it you don't understand?"

"I thought I was riding towards the canal . . . So how can it be that I . . ."

Comrade Kondratiev said nothing for a minute or two and then quietly put down the receiver.

I switched on Radio Beacon—I didn't believe it was really Beacon, even though every two minutes they assured me it was.

"Maria Ivanovna Plakhuta from the village of Nukino has given the Motherland seven sons," said a woman's voice, soaring out over the factory lunchtime in distant Russia. "Two of them, Ivan Plakhuta and Vassily Plakhuta, are now serving in the army, in the tank forces of the KGB. They have asked us to broadcast the comic song 'The Samovar' for their mother. We're doing just as you asked, lads. Maria Ivanovna, here singing for you is People's Jester of the USSR, Artem Plakhuta, who was just as delighted to accept our invitation as he was to be demobilised from the army with the rank of senior sergeant eight years before his brothers."

Then the balalaikas began to jangle, the cymbals clashed a couple of times, and a voice filled with feeling, leaning hard on the letter *r* as if it were the person crushed next to him in a crowded bus, began to sing:
"O-oh, the wa-terr's on the boil!"

I switched it off. The words sent a shiver through me.
I remembered Dima's grey head and the cow on the
cover of *Atom Heart Mother*, and a cold shudder ran
slowly down my spine. I waited a minute or two until I
was sure the song must have finished, and turned the
black knob. For a second there was silence, and then
the baritone leapt out of hiding straight into my face
with:

> *We gave the skunks our tea to drink,*
> *Fed them water fiery hot!*

This time I waited longer, and when I finally
switched the radio on, the announcer was speaking.
"Let us remember our cosmonauts, and all those
whose earthly labours make possible their shift-work in
the heavens. For them today . . ."
I withdrew into my own thoughts, or rather, I suddenly found myself immersed in one of them, as though
I had fallen through thin ice, and I only began to hear
anything again a few minutes later, as a ponderous
choir of distant basses was laying the final bricks in the
monumental edifice of a new song. But even though I
was completely unaware of the real world, I carried on
mechanically pressing the pedals, with my right knee
turned out as far as possible—that way I felt less pain
from the blister my boot had given me.
I was struck by a sudden idea.
If now, when I closed my eyes, I was—as far as a person can actually be anywhere—on a phantom highway
outside Moscow, and the nonexistent asphalt, trees, and
sunshine became as real to me as though I actually was

dashing down a slope in my favourite second gear; if—
forgetting about Zabriskie Point, which was not very far
off now—I was sometimes happy for a few seconds,
didn't that mean that already back then in my childhood, when I was simply a part of a world submerged
in summer happiness, when I really was dashing along
the asphalt strip on my bicycle, riding against the wind
into the sun, without the slightest interest in what the
future had in store for me—didn't that mean that even
then I was really already trundling across the black, lifeless surface of the moon, seeing nothing but what pene-
trated into consciousness through the crooked spy holes
as the moonwalker slowly solidified around me?

> We're spaceward bound tomorrow
> But there's no grief or sorrow
> Alone in the sky.
> The moon's riding high.
> You ripe ears of barley, goodbye.

I saw a board on the wall bearing a pointy-bearded golden profile and the word "Lenin", written in a semicircle and framed by two metal-foil olive branches. Although I'd walked past the spot plenty of times before, there had always been people around, and I hadn't dared go right up close.

I scanned the entire structure with a new interest: the board was quite large—about a metre high—and covered with crimson velvet. It hung from two hinges, and a small hook on the back held it right up against the wall. I glanced around. Quiet hour wasn't over yet, and there was no one in the corridor. I went over to the window—the avenue leading to the dining hall was empty, except for two moonwalkers at the far end, slowly creeping towards me. I recognised the camp leaders, Kolya and Lena. It was quiet, the only sound was the tapping of a table-tennis ball downstairs: I was filled with melancholy at the idea that someone had the right to play table tennis during the quiet hour. Then I unlatched the hook and pulled the board towards me, revealing a square section of the wall. Right in the centre of it I saw a switch, painted with gold paint. The hollow churning in the pit of my stomach grew even worse as I reached out and flicked the switch upwards.

There was a low buzzing sound. Without even knowing what it was, I felt like I'd done something terrible to
the world around me, and to myself as well. The buzzer
sounded again, louder this time, and suddenly I realised
that the switch, the small crimson door I'd opened, and
the corridor I was standing in—none of it was real, because I wasn't really standing by a switch on a wall but
sitting uncomfortably hunched over in some terribly
cramped space. There was another buzz, and a few seconds later the moonwalker materialised around me. One
more buzz, and the thought flitted through my mind
that yesterday, before I lowered my head onto the
handlebars, I had extended the red line on the map to
the centre of the black circle beside the words "Zabriskie Point".

The phone was ringing.

"Sleep well, you asshole?" Colonel Khalmuradov's
voice thundered in the receiver.

"Asshole yourself," I said, suddenly angry.

Khalmuradov gave a rumbling, infectious laugh—I
realised he wasn't offended at all.

"I'm all alone again here in Central Flight Control.
The lads have gone off to Japan to set up a joint flight
mission. Pkhadzer Vladlenovich sends you his regards,
says he was sorry he didn't get to say goodbye—it was
all decided at the last moment. And I had to stay here
all because of you. Well, are you setting up the radio
buoy today? Probably had enough, have you? Glad it's
over?"

I didn't answer.

"What's this, are you angry with me? Omon? Just because I called you a wanker that time? Forget it, will

you? You had all Central Flight Control shitting bricks, we almost had to cancel the flight," said Khalmuradov. He paused, then went on. "You act just like a stupid woman . . . Are you a man or not? Today's a special day. Just you remember that."

"I remember," I said.

"Button yourself up as tight as you can," Khalmuradov advised me anxiously, "especially the neck of your jacket. Your face . . ."

"I know what to do as well as you," I interrupted.

"First you put on the goggles, then you wrap the scarf round your head, and then you put on your cap. Be sure to fasten it under your chin. Then the gloves. Tie your sleeves and your boots with string—you can't mess around with a vacuum. Then you'll be able to last three minutes. Understood?"

"Understood."

"Not 'understood', you bastard—'yes, sir'. Report back when you're ready."

They say that during the last minutes of his life a man sees it all again in fast rewind. I don't know about that. Nothing of the sort happened to me, no matter how hard I tried. What I saw instead was a vivid, strangely detailed picture of Landratov in Japan—walking along the street in the morning sunshine wearing brand-new expensive training shoes and smiling—probably not even remembering what kind of feet he was wearing them on. And I imagined the others—the Flight Leader transformed into an elderly intellectual in a three-piece suit, and Comrade Kondratiev giving a thoughtful interview to a correspondent from the television current-affairs programme. But not a single thought about myself entered my head. To calm myself down, I switched on the radio and listened to a quiet song about lights burning in the distance beyond the river, a head lowered in sorrow, a heart pierced by grief, and White Guards who had nothing to lose but their golden watch chains.

Suddenly the radio was switched off and the phone rang.

"Well," asked Khalmuradov, "are you ready?"

"Not yet," I answered, "what's the hurry?"

"You little jerk, you," said Khalmuradov, "I saw what it said in your personal file about you not having any childhood friends except for that bastard we shot. Don't you ever think about other people? I could miss my tennis again."

Somehow I found it incredibly offensive to think that in a short while Khalmuradov would be standing on the courts at Luzhniki with white shorts on his fat thighs, knocking a tennis ball around the asphalt, while I wouldn't be around anymore. I didn't feel this because I envied him but because I suddenly recalled with startling clarity a certain sunny September day in that same Luzhniki, when I was still at school. But then I realised that when I was gone, Khalmuradov and Luzhniki itself would be gone too, and the thought dispelled the melancholy my dream had left with me.

"Other people? What other people?" I asked quietly. "Anyway, it's no big deal. You go. I'll manage on my own."

"Stop that."

"It's all right, you go."

"Stop it, stop it," Khalmuradov said in a serious

voice. "I have to finalise the report, register the signal from the moon, note the time in Moscow. Just you get on with it."

"Is Landratov in Japan too?" I suddenly asked.

"What's that you asked?" Khalmuradov said suspiciously.

"I just remembered something."

"So, what was it you remembered? Tell me."

"I just remembered him dancing the 'Kalinka' at the graduation exams."

"I get you. Hey, Landratov, are you in Japan? Some-one here's asking for you."

There was a sound of laughter and the slippery squeak of fingers on the receiver.

"He's here," Khalmuradov said at last. "He sends his regards."

"Give him mine too. All right, I suppose it's time."

"Push open the hatch," Khalmuradov said quickly, repeating the instructions I knew by heart, "and imme-diately grab the handlebars so the air pressure won't throw you out. Then take a breath from the oxygen mask through the scarf and climb out. Walk fifteen steps along the line of motion, take out the radio buoy, set it down, and turn it on. Make sure you carry it a good distance, or the moonwalker will screen the signal . . . And then . . . We've given you a pistol with a single bullet, and we've never had any cowards in the cosmo-nauts' detachment yet."

I hung up. The telephone rang again, but I took no notice. For a second I toyed with the idea of not switch-ing on the radio buoy so that bastard Khalmuradov would have to hang around in Central Flight Control till the end of the day, and then collect some kind of Party reprimand, but I remembered Sema Anikin and how he said I had to get there and finish the job. I couldn't betray the guys from the first and second stages, not even unsociable Dima; they'd died so I could be here now, and in the face of their exalted destiny my spiteful feelings for Khalmuradov seemed petty and shameful. And when I finally knew that in a few seconds I would gather my courage and do what had to be done, the phone stopped ringing.

I began making preparations, and in half an hour I was ready. I sealed my ears and nostrils tightly with the special hydrocompensatory tampons made of greased cotton wool and then checked my outfit—everything was buttoned up tight, tucked in and tied down; the rubber strap of the motorcycle goggles was a little too tight, and they bit into my face, but I didn't try fiddling with them: I wouldn't have to put up with it for very long anyway. I picked up the holster from the shelf, drew out the pistol, cocked it, and shoved it into the pocket of my padded jacket. I threw the sack with the radio buoy over my left shoulder, and was just about to pick up the phone when I remembered I'd already sealed my ears with cotton wool; and anyway, I didn't really want to waste my final moments of life on conversation with Khalmuradov. I remembered the last time I talked to Dima and I was sure I had done the right thing by lying to him about *Zabriskie Point*. It's a miserable thing to leave behind a world which still holds secrets.

I breathed out, as though I were about to jump into deep water, and set to work.

After all those hours of training, my body knew what it had to do so well that I didn't stop once, even though I had to work in almost total darkness, because the battery was so weak the lamp had stopped giving out light —I could just make out the little crimson worm of the filament. First I had to remove five bolts around the edge of the hatch. When the final bolt clanged against the floor, I felt along the wall for the little window over the emergency opening switch and hit the glass hard with my last can of corned beef. The glass shattered. I stuck my hand in through the opening, hooked my finger into the ring of the explosive cartridge, and tugged. The cartridge was made with explosives from an F-1 grenade, and it had a three-second delay, so there was just enough time for me to grab the handlebars and get my head down as low as possible. There was a thunderous bang above my head and I was shaken so hard I was almost thrown out of the saddle, but I managed to hold on. I waited half a second and raised my head.

There above me was the black bottomless abyss of open space. The only thing between me and it was the thin Plexiglas of my motorcycle goggles. I was surrounded by total darkness. I bent down, took a deep breath from the oxygen mask, scrambled clumsily out of the moonwalker, stood up, and began walking—every step cost an immense effort to overcome the pain in my back, which I hadn't straightened up for a month. I didn't feel like walking the full fifteen steps, so I went down on one knee, loosened the string around the sack with the radio buoy, and started pulling it out, but the lever got jammed and I couldn't shift it. It was getting

harder and harder to hold the air in my lungs, and I
had a brief moment of panic—I thought I would die
there and then, without finishing the job I had come to
do. But the next moment the sack slipped off; I set the
radio buoy on the invisible surface of the moon and
turned the lever. Out into the ether flew the encoded
words "Lenin", "USSR", and "Peace", repeated every
three seconds, and a tiny red lamp sprang to life on the
side of the buoy, lighting up an image of the earth floating across ears of barley—and for the first time in my
life I noticed that my Motherland's national emblem
showed the view from the moon.

The air was bursting out of my lungs, and I knew in a
few seconds I would let it go and my scorched mouth
would choke on emptiness. I swung back my arm and
threw the nickel-plated bed knob as far as I could. It
was time to die. I took the pistol out of my pocket,
raised it to my temple, and tried to remember the most
important event of my brief existence, but the only
thing that came into my head was the story of Marat Popadya as his father had told it to me. I was offended by
the absurdity of dying with a thought that had nothing
to do with me, and I tried to think of something else,
but I couldn't; I could see the clearing in the winter forest, the huntsmen sitting in the bushes, the two bears
roaring as they rushed at the hunters—and as I pressed
the trigger, I suddenly realised beyond a shadow of a
doubt that Kissinger had very well known what he was
stabbing at.

The pistol misfired, but it wasn't needed anyway;
there were bright-coloured lifebelts drifting in front of

my eyes; I tried to grab one of them, missed, and col-
lapsed onto the black, ice-cold lunar basalt.

•

I felt a sharp stone sticking into my cheek—it wasn't all
that painful through the scarf, but it was unpleasant
enough. I propped myself up on my elbows and looked
around. I could not see a thing. My nose began to itch; I
sneezed, and one of the tampons flew out of my nostril.
Then I pulled off the scarf, the goggles, and the cap and
dragged the swollen cotton-wool tampons out of my
ears and nose. I couldn't hear anything, but there was a
distinct musty smell. It was damp and cold—despite
the padded jacket.

I stood up and fumbled round about me, then
stretched out my arms and started walking forward. Almost immediately I stumbled over something, but I kept
my balance. A few steps later my fingers came up
against a wall; I moved my hands along it and felt a
thick festoon of wires covered in sticky fluff. I turned
and walked in the opposite direction, walking more
carefully this time, lifting my feet high in the air, but after a few steps I stumbled over something again. Again
my hands felt a wall with cables hanging on it. Then I
noticed a tiny red lamp lighting up a five-sided metal
object about five metres away from me—and I remembered everything.

But before I could come to terms with what I remembered or think clearly about anything, there was a flash
of light far off to my right; I turned my head, instinc-
tively shielding my face with my hands, and through
the gaps between my fingers I saw a tunnel running off

into the distance—the bright light was at the far end of it, and it lit up the thick bunches of cables covering the walls and the rails that ran together in a distant point.

Turning away from the light, I saw the moonwalker standing on the rails, painted all over in stars and emblazoned with the letters USSR, and my own long black shadow falling across it. I stumbled towards it, shielding my face from the blinding light drifting towards me above the rails—somehow it suddenly reminded me of the setting sun. Something ricocheted off the fuselage of the moonwalker at the very same instant as I heard a loud crack; I realised I was being shot at and made a dash for shelter behind the moonwalker. Another bullet clanged against the fuselage, and it went on ringing for several seconds, like a funeral bell. I heard the clatter of wheels, then there was another shot, and the clattering of wheels stopped.

"Hey, Krivomazov!" thundered an inhumanly loud voice. "Come out with your hands up, you bastard! They've given you a medal!"

I peeped out from behind the moonwalker: standing on the rails about fifty metres away was a small hand trolley with a blinding searchlight, and swaying to and fro in front of it on wide-straddled legs was a man with a megaphone in one hand and a pistol in the other. He raised the gun: a shot rang out like thunder and the bullet ricocheted several times before it whistled past just below the roof. I hid my head.

"Come on out, you skunk!"

His voice was familiar, but I couldn't quite tell who it was.

"Two!"

He fired again, and hit the fuselage of the moonwalker.

"Three!"

I peeped out again and saw him put the megaphone on his trolley, stretch out his arms to the sides, and begin to jog slowly over the sleepers towards the moonwalker. When he got a bit closer, I could hear him making buzzing noises with his mouth, imitating the roar of aeroplane engines, and I recognised him straightaway—it was Landratov. I would have backed away down the tunnel, but I realised that as soon as he reached the moonwalker, I would be absolutely defenceless. I hesitated for a second, then bent down and dived under the low hull.

All I could see now were his legs coming closer and closer, stepping deftly but somehow sloppily over the sleepers. He didn't seem to have noticed anything. When he got close to the moonwalker, he began buzzing differently, with a more intense sound, and I realised he was banking steeply as he rounded the machine. His boot appeared between the rusty wheels, and without having planned it, I grabbed his legs. When my fingers closed around his ankles, the sensation of almost total emptiness in his boots was so nauseating I nearly let go of them again. He shouted and fell. I didn't loosen my grip, and the artificial limbs twisted unnaturally in the soft leather. I gave them one more twist and crawled out from under the moonwalker; by the time I was free of it, he was already crawling towards his pistol, which had fallen between the sleepers. I had only a second left; I grabbed the heavy five-sided radio buoy and smashed it down on the back of Landratov's yellow-haired head.

There was a crunching sound, and the little red lamp went out.

•

Landratov's hand trolley was a lot lighter than my moonwalker and it moved a lot faster. The powerful searchlight lit up the round gallery and the cables running along its walls, all with a sticky covering of some kind of tacky fibres. As far as I could tell, the gallery was an abandoned metro tunnel. At several points other tunnels branched off from it, just as dark and lifeless as the one I was travelling along. Occasionally rats ran across ahead—some of them were as big as small dogs—but they paid no attention to me, thank God. Then came a side tunnel on the right, just like the others, but as I got close, the trolley jerked so sharply to the right that I flew off onto the rails and bruised my shoulder badly.

The points I'd just ridden over were set in a halfway position, so that the front wheels went straight ahead while the back wheels went to the right; as a result, the trolley was jammed solid. I knew I had to go on in the darkness on foot, and I began slowly feeling my way forward, regretting that I hadn't picked up Landratov's pistol, though it would hardly have saved me from the rats if they decided to attack.

Before I'd gone fifty metres I heard shouting and dogs barking ahead of me. I turned and ran back the way I'd come. Lights came on behind me; turning to look, I saw the grey forms of two Alsatians leaping over the sleepers ahead of the swaying circles of torchlight which were all I could see of my pursuers.

"There he is! Belka! Strelka! Get him!" someone yelled behind me.

I turned into the side tunnel and set off as fast as I could, striding high so I wouldn't break my legs. I stepped on a rat and almost fell; then suddenly I saw the bright unwinking points of unearthly stars shining off to my right. I dashed towards them, collided with a wall, and clambered over it, clutching at the cables, and all the while feeling the Alsatians rushing at my back. I tumbled over the top of the wall and fell, and the only reason I didn't hurt myself was that I landed on something very soft, which felt like an armchair covered in polythene. I squeezed into a crevice between some boxes and crates and began creeping along it; several times my hands knocked against the backs of chairs and the arms of armchairs wrapped in polythene. Suddenly it was brighter. I heard a quiet conversation very close by and I froze. Right in front of my face was the back panel of a wardrobe—a large sheet of hardboard with the word "Nevka" stamped on it. I heard barks and shouting behind me, and then a loud voice amplified by a megaphone:

"Stop that! Quiet! We're on the air in two minutes!"

The dogs carried on barking, and an insolent tenor voice tried to explain what the problem was, but the megaphone started roaring again:

"Fuck off out of here if you and your dogs don't want to be court-martialled!"

The barking gradually faded—obviously the dogs had

been dragged away. After a minute I felt brave enough
to peek out from behind the wardrobe.

At first I thought I must be in some huge ancient Roman planetarium. On an immensely high vaulted ceiling, set among glass and tin, the distant stars glimmered
at about one-third of full voltage. About forty metres
from the wardrobe stood an old crane; attached to its
lifting arm, about four metres above the ground, was a
Salyut spacecraft, shaped like a huge bottle. Docked
with the Salyut was an Agdam T-3 cargo shuttle; the
spaceship sat on the lifting arm the way a plastic model
aeroplane sits on its stand. The entire structure was obviously too heavy for the crane to support, because the
stern of the cargo shuttle was supported by a couple of
long beams braced against the floor; I could just make
them out in the half-light, but when two floodlights
came on right beside the wardrobe, they became almost
invisible because, like the wall behind them, they were
painted black and covered with pieces of glittering foil
that reflected the electric light.

The floodlights were fitted with filters, and their light
was a strange, deathly white. Apart from the spaceship,
which immediately looked very convincing, they also lit
up a television camera and two machine-gunners who
were smoking beside it, and a long table with micro-
phones, food, and spectrally transparent bottles of
vodka looking like icicles that had been hammered
through the table; sitting at the table were two generals.
At one side stood a table with a microphone, at which a
man in civilian clothes was sitting. Behind him was
a large sheet of plywood with the word "News" and a
drawing of the earth; rising crookedly over the earth

was a five-pointed star with long, extended side rays.
Another civilian was leaning over the table and talking
to the man behind the microphone.

"Double three!"

I didn't see who said that. The second civilian ran
over to the camera and pointed it towards the small table. A bell rang, and the man at the microphone began
to speak:

"Today we are at the front line of Soviet space science, in one of the branches of Central Flight Control.
Cosmonauts Armen Vezirov and Djambul Mezhelaitis
are now in their seventh year on board an orbital spacecraft. This is the longest space flight in history, and it
has put our country at the forefront of world space technology. It is symbolic that I should be here with camera-
man Nikolai Gordienko on the very day when the
cosmonauts are carrying out an important scientific
assignment—in exactly thirty seconds they will emerge
from their craft into open space in order to install the
Quantum astrophysics module."

The entire space was suddenly illuminated by a soft,
diffused light—I raised my head and saw that the lamps
on the ceiling had been turned up to full voltage, revealing a magnificent panorama of the starry sky to
which man has aspired for so many centuries, the inspi-
ration for those beautiful but naïve legends about silver
nails driven into the firmament.

There was the sound of muffled blows from the direction of the Salyut—the sound of a shoulder hammering
on a cellar door which is swollen from damp, when the
person opening it is afraid of overturning the pots of
sour cream just inside. Finally I saw the door of the

hatch projecting slightly above the fuselage of the spaceship, and the man at the table with the microphone
spoke:

"Attention, we're going live!"

The hatch slowly opened, and a round silvery helmet
with a short antenna appeared above the side of the
spaceship. Everyone at the table applauded; the helmet
was followed by shoulders and a pair of silvery arms—
the first thing they did was attach a safety line to the
special bracket on the fuselage; their movements were
very slow and smooth, perfected by long hours of training in the swimming pool. Finally the first cosmonaut
clambered out into open space and stopped a few steps
away from the hatch. I thought it must take quite a lot
of courage to stand like that four metres above the
ground. Then I had the impression that one of the generals at the table was looking in my direction, and I
pulled my head in behind the wardrobe. When I shoved
it back out again, both cosmonauts were standing on the
spaceship, their suits blindingly white against the inky-
black background of the cosmic abyss, scattered with
the tiny points of stars. One of them was holding a
small box; the cosmonauts moved with a slow, under-
water gait along the fuselage of the spaceship to a tall
mast and quickly screwed the box to it. Then they
turned to face the television cameras, waved their hands
smoothly, walked back to the hatch with that same un-
derwater stride, and one after the other disappeared
inside.

The hatch closed, but I went on staring at the stars
glittering so unimaginably far away—at the long, slim
arms of the constellation of the Swan, uncertain whether

to embrace the huge Pegasus which covered half the
sky, or the small but touchingly pure and clear Lyra.

The man in civilian clothes was speaking rapidly and
happily into his microphone:

"While the operation was in progress there was silence here at Central Flight Control. I must confess I
was holding my breath too, but everything went according to plan. One has to marvel at the cosmonauts' precision and coordination—the years of training and orbital
flight have clearly not been wasted. The scientific
equipment installed today . . ."

I crept behind the wardrobe. I felt apathetic, indifferent to everything. If they had tried to catch me then,
I probably wouldn't have bothered to run for it or
even resist; the only thing I wanted to do was sleep.
Following my moonside habit, I rested my head on my
folded arms and dozed off. Through my sleep I heard a
voice:

"This television broadcast of men at work in open
space came from a camera installed by the flight engi-
neer on one of the main unit's solar batteries."

•

I slept for a long time, maybe five hours. A few times
someone began moving things around and swearing
close by, then a thin female voice said the divan had to
be changed, but I didn't budge—I could have been
dreaming. When I finally came round, everything was
quiet. I stood up cautiously and glanced out from behind the wardrobe. There was no one at the table with
the microphone, and the television camera was covered
with a groundsheet. One floodlight lit up the spaceship.

I couldn't see anyone there. I came out from behind the wardrobe and looked around: everything was just the same as during the television broadcast, but now I noticed there was quite a large pile of garbage under the spaceship—horrible scraps of white paper and empty tins.

I went over to the table, to the leftover vodka and plates of hors d'oeuvres; I wanted a drink badly. When I sat down, my back automatically hunched over into the bicycle posture; I straightened up with considerable effort and poured all the leftover vodka together—there was enough for two full glasses, and I drank them down one after the other. For several seconds I thought about following them with one of the marinated mushrooms left on the plate, but the sight of a fork covered in sticky slime made me feel squeamish.

I remembered my crewmates, and imagined a hall like this one, with zinc coffins standing on the floor—four soldered shut and one still empty. I supposed in some ways the others were happier than I, but I still felt sad for them. Then I thought about Mitiok. Pretty soon I got this buzzing in my head, and I found I could think about what had happened that day. But instead of doing that, I remembered my last day on earth, with the rain darkening the cobblestones on Red Square, Colonel Urchagin's wheelchair, and his warm lips brushing my ear as he whispered:

"I know how hard it was for you to lose your friend and learn that ever since you were a child you had been approaching your moment of immortality arm in arm with a cunning and experienced enemy—I won't even pronounce his name. But remember a certain conversation at which the three of us were present, when he said: 'What does it matter what thought a man dies with? We're materialists, after all.' You remember I said that after he dies a man lives on in the fruit of his deeds. But there is something else I didn't say, something even more important. Remember, Omon, although man, of course, has no soul, every soul is a universe. That's the dialectic. And as long as there is a single soul in which our cause lives and conquers, that cause will never die. For an entire universe will exist, and at its centre will be this . . ."

He gestured across the square, where the cobblestones gleamed, black and menacing.

"And now for the most important thing you must remember, Omon. You can't understand what I'm going to say yet, but I'm saying it for a moment that will come later, when I won't be beside you. So listen. Just one pure and honest soul is enough for our country to take the lead in the conquest of space; just one pure soul is enough for the banner of triumphant socialism to be unfurled on the surface of the distant moon. But there must be one pure soul, if only for a moment, because the banner will be unfurled within that soul . . ."

Suddenly I caught a powerful smell of sweat and started to turn around, only to be knocked from my chair by a blow from a fist in a thick rubber glove.

A figure towered over me in a tattered felt spacesuit and a helmet with the letters USSR painted on its rim in red. He grabbed an empty bottle, smashed it against the table, and leaned down over me with the jagged edge in his raised hand; I managed to roll away, jump to my feet, and run for it. He set off after me—although his movements were very slow, he still managed to move very fast, in a way that was terrifying. I spotted his companion out of the corner of my eye—he was hurriedly clambering down one of the black beams propping up the Agdam T-3, knocking off the tinfoil stars as he went. I ran to the doors and charged them with my shoulder, but they were locked. I ran back and dodged past the first cosmonaut, only to run straight into the second, who swung his leg and kicked at me with a boot with a heavy magnetic sole. He aimed for the groin but hit me on the leg—and then tried to butt me in the stomach with the sharp antenna on his helmet. I managed to dodge away again. It was then I realised I'd drunk the vodka they had probably been looking forward to for years, and I felt really scared. Ahead of me I saw a small door with the word DANGER painted on it, and a bolt of lightning inside a triangle. I ran for it.

Behind the door was a very narrow corridor with a rumbling iron floor. I forced myself to run about five metres along it, and then I heard again the heavy clanging of magnetic soles behind my back. That gave me speed and strength: I turned a corner and saw a short corridor ending in the round opening of a ventilation shaft with its wire grille torn away. Beyond the opening stood a motionless rusty fan blade. As I turned to run back, I was so close to my pursuer I didn't even sense him as a single whole, just a collection of unrelated impressions: a sphere with a bottle-green Plexiglas visor and huge red letters, a black rubber glove with a small transparent trident protruding from it, a powerful smell of sweat, and a major's epaulettes on silver-painted felt. The next instant I was already squirming into the ventilation shaft behind the wire netting; I squeezed pretty quickly between the blades of the huge fan, like a ship's propeller, but when I began climbing into the shaft that led upwards and away, my padded jacket bunched up and I got stuck there, squirming like an embryo in the womb. There was a rustling sound below me and something touched my ankle. I shouted and jerked myself free and upwards, covering two metres in a matter of seconds and then squeezing into a horizontal branch of the shaft. It ended in a round opening, and beyond that I could see the earth swathed in wispy clouds; I sobbed and crawled towards it.

Through the film of my tears the earth was blurred and indistinct, and it seemed to be suspended in a yellowish void; I watched its surface draw closer from out of this void as I squirmed my way towards it, until the walls that were pressing in on me parted and the brown tiles of the floor flew up to meet me.

•

"Hey you, mister!" I opened my eyes. A woman in a dirty blue smock was bending over me; a bucket stood on the floor beside her, and she had a mop in her hand.

"Feeling bad, are you? What d'you want here?"

I looked around me—in the wall opposite me there was a small brown door. Beside it hung a calendar with a big photograph of the earth and the words "For Peace in Space!" I was lying in a short corridor with blue-painted walls, with three or four doors close by. Looking up, I saw the black opening of a ventilation shaft in the wall opposite the calendar.

"Eh?" I asked.

"I said, you drunk, are you?"

Supporting myself against the wall, I got to my feet and set off along the corridor.

"Where d'you think you're going?" the woman said, and turned me round roughly. I set off in the opposite direction. Around the corner there was a steep staircase leading upwards, which ended in a wooden door. Beyond the door there was an indistinct buzz of noise.

"Go on," said the woman, pushing me from behind.

I walked up the steps and then looked round—she was watching me carefully from the bottom of the stairs. I pushed the door and found myself standing in a dark niche behind several people in civilian clothes. They took no notice of me. There was a distant rumbling sound, gradually growing louder. Glancing sideways, I read an inscription in bronze letters—LENIN LIBRARY.

The thought suddenly hit me—earth!

I stepped out of the cubbyhole under the stairs and staggered slowly along the metro platform towards the large mirror at its far end. Above the mirror menacing orange digits spelled out the time, informing me that it was not yet evening but time was getting on and the previous train had passed through just over four minutes ago. The face of a young man with stubble that hadn't seen a razor in ages was staring at me out of the mirror; his eyes were inflamed and his hair was a tangled mess. He was wearing a dirty black padded jacket, smeared in places with whitewash, and he looked as though he'd spent last night far from a bed.

A policeman with a small moustache who was striding up and down the hall began giving me the eye, and when a train arrived and the doors opened, I stepped in through the opening without a second thought. The doors closed, and the train carried me off into a new life. The flight continues, I thought. Half the lamps in the moonwalker weren't working, which sort of soured the light. I sat down; the woman beside me automatically squeezed her legs together, moved away from me, and set her string shopping bag in the space between us. From the corner of my eye I noticed a box of macaroni stars and the sad, small shape of a frozen chicken.

•

I had to decide where to go. I looked up at the metro diagram on the wall beside the emergency-stop handle, and began to work out where exactly on the red line I was.

Moscow, 1992